DEAD WORLD

LUCAS PEDERSON

SEVERED PRESS
HOBART TASMANIA

DEAD WORLD

ISBN: 978-1-925711-70-7

ONE

Somewhere in the darkness, water drips, echoing off the stone walls of the tunnel. The sound mingles with the shuffling of boots.

The tepid air reeks. Like a bushel of rotting tomatoes.

Dr. Alyx Wick adjusts the filter scarf over her mouth and nose. The scans don't indicate anything toxic, but she's come to rely more on instincts rather than technology. Hasn't failed her yet.

The lights barely penetrate the absolute darkness of the tunnel ahead. Cuts off at about thirty feet.

Behind her, Morris mutters an old Xyeth prayer. He's new to her team, inexperienced and jittery. So far, he hasn't shown much of anything besides fear. Which is a dangerous thing during explorations. Fear puts everyone else in jeopardy. It clouds the mind. Still, she needs his knowledge of the Xyeth tunnels. She knows about them, but only from old books. She brought Morris on as a guide, mostly. His other abilities, well…she'll see if he was lying sooner or later.

A shrill cry from down the tunnel bounces off the walls, batters Alyx's ears.

Morris sucks in a sharp breath, all those prayers dying in his flabby throat.

Alyx's free hand drifts to the butt of the gun on her hip.

"Dahs bad sign," Morris mumbles.

Alyx rolls her eyes, glances at him over her shoulder. "Shh."

"No," he says. "I not go now. We turn back."

"I'm paying you to guide me to the Sythilias. You tuck tail and run now, our deal is off." And when he grumbles something about not being paid enough, Alyx spins on him. He stumbles away in surprise. Em and Crane catch him before he falls. She nods at Em and Crane, the only two in the Universe she really trusts, and they let Morris go.

He, with his scaly, reptilian skin, rights his filter scarf and glares at Alyx with double lidded yellow eyes. "Too dangerous, don't you see? Bad things in tunnels."

"You said that before we left."

"Tis true! Shoulda never came here."

Alyx, smirking, steps closer to Morris. He's shorter than her by about three inches, but what he lacks in height, he makes up for in stoutness. He's like a walking boulder. And Xyeths are renowned for their superior strength. Even so, Morris lowers his lizard-like head, double lids blinking.

"You said whatever used to live in the tunnels were long dead." Alyx grabs Morris's scarf and yanks him close. "So, what the hell did we just hear?"

Morris, snout exposed now, thin lips quivering to reveal small, pointy teeth, simply blinks at her.

Alyx yanks him closer, nearly nose to snout. "What did we *hear*?"

"I-I-I...I dunno, Dr. Wick. Things in here. Sacred place. Shoulda stayed away."

She shoves him away, sight darting from Em to Crane. "Be ready."

They nod in tandem and draw their guns. Revolvers loaded with lumini rounds. Bullets able to take down the largest of beasts.

Or so Alyx hopes.

She bends to Morris, about to ask him for the map, when a low, rumbling growl trembles the air behind her. Morris, gasping, backing away as Em and Wick step around him, eyes focused on whatever growls behind her.

Heart whipping against the walls of her chest, Alyx's hand slips to the gun on her hip. She whirls around, dropping low, and pulling the trigger in a single fluid motion. Em and Crane fire their weapons a second later, lighting up the darkness.

She catches a few glimpses of something large with tight, white skin and massive snapping yellow teeth before the gun flashes go out. All the lights are pointed at the floor. The creature howls, something swishes through the air directly in front of Alyx, blowing her hat off. She grabs it, slaps it back on her head and points the gun at a wall of black.

"Lights," she shouts.

There's a click and the tunnel is doused in high density, white light.

Long, yellow teeth snap an inch from her face. Greenish blood dribbles out of three holes in the monster's broad chest. It drops to all fours, roars at her. Three black eyes sunken in the white flesh of its narrow face, glare at her. Blue drool slathers the stone floor under it. It squeals, as if the light hurts it. The creature slaps its claws inches from her boots, yet doesn't attack.

"Well," Alyx says, "you're an ugly bastard, aren't ya."

She points the gun at the creature's head, squeezes the trigger. *Sklack*. Half of the narrow head explodes in a splatter of green and yellow. The monster chuffs, staggers to the right, and collapses.

Steadying her breathing, Alyx stands, holsters the gun and turns to Em and Crane. Both are humans and they blink at her. Em looks like he's about to say something when she waves him away. Her sight shifts around the two men.

"Where's Morris?"

"Sucker ran off," Crane says in his deep voice.

"Gave me this, though," Em says and hands Alyx a slim, clear sheet of hard plastic.

The map.

Lips forming a thin, white line on her sweaty face, Alyx taps the sheet and immediately the map pops up. A green circle shows her their location. She turns, facing down the tunnel. A small, red X marks their destination.

Over her shoulder, she says, "Let's go."

She steps over the dead creature and continues down the tunnel. Behind her, Em and Crane follow without a word. Em has been with her since the early days on Earth, before that planet choked and died. There are no more mysteries left to find on Earth. All artefacts have been discovered and those still lost...well, they'll remain lost. Earth's artefacts aren't worth much anyway these days.

Building her reputation for finding the unfindable, Alyx brought Em along for the intergalactic ride. Crane came only a couple years later while on an exploration of the ghost planet Pluto. He'd been with another team searching for precious metals and joined Alyx once she revealed his employers had no idea what they were doing.

Trust...it's an important thing.

Perhaps the rarest of things.

The tunnel turns left, then right before finally coming to a T. Alyx, following the map, takes the right tunnel, which begins to gradually taper inward. The deeper she goes, the lower the ceiling becomes, the more the walls close in. Her shoulders scrape against the damp stone so she begins walking sideways, sparing a glance behind. Em isn't having much of a problem, but Crane is. He's almost seven feet tall and two hundred-eighty pounds. The man is a behemoth and walking through this tunnel, Alyx notes, is turning into a major task. At least he's not claustrophobic. Poor guy. She almost tells him to wait for them, then thinks better of it. Crane is the type of guy who'll push onward, despite the difficulties. An admirable, but frustrating trait.

The problem isn't the creatures stalking the tunnels, but what lies ahead. That's if what's in the books are true. Sometimes stories are only stories. But...

The narrow tunnel opens to a small room. The walls are shrouded with cobwebs. At the center of the room is a silver circle. It glitters in the lights thrown by Em and Crane.

Em starts forward, about to cross the threshold into the room and Alyx stops him.

"Stay here," she says.

Em backs up a few feet, nodding.

Alyx returns her attention to the room. Her eyes shift back and forth, up and down, sight picking out any abnormalities. The walls, with their swaths of cobwebs, doesn't make much sense. Unless they are the remnants of spiders now long extinct. It's possible. And yet...

A frown creases on her face as she stares at the right wall.

Nothing in the texts, nor the tid-bits of information from Morris, ever mentioned spiders.

On the other side of the room awaits the entrances of two other tunnels. According to the map, she needs to take the left one. But, if memory serves right, this is the Room of Tangles. Where nothing is what it seems. Then again, texts aren't always true facts. Still, if nothing is what it seems, then the webs aren't really webs, but something else. And the tunnels...

She fixes her sight on the circle drawn into the middle of the floor. More like etched.

"Dr. Wick?"

She looks over her shoulder at Crane.

"Morris said something about this room. He said the room with the circle will kill us all."

Alyx snorts. "They all say that." But when she turns back to the room, her eyes widen a bit and she blows out a long breath. She wipes sweat from her face and focuses on the circle.

There's something about the circle. Something that teeters on the edge of her mind. But what? Damn it. What...

She smiles, snaps her fingers and spins on Em. The guy just about jumps out of his pants. "The stones!"

Em, blinking, manages, "Huh?"

Alyx reaches out. "The West Wood stones in the pack. Give'em to me."

Em shrugs out of the pack and begins rummaging through it.

"Hurry," Alyx says.

He brings out a small, black sack. The contents click as he hands it over. Alyx grabs it, swings back to the room and opens the sack. Inside are three luminous stones. All glow a deep purple. The West Wood stones are relics said to set things that are askew to true. She's been carrying them for years, but until now has never tried them out. If this truly is the Room of Tangles, the stones should show her what's real and what's not.

The stones are about the size of golf balls, shaped like eggs. Alyx tosses one near the right wall. The stone flickers. Darker purple shifts to lighter purple, to an almost pink color. She waits, keeping her sight on the wall blanketed in webs. Light bursts out of the stone, glaring in every direction, and when it subsides, the wall is gone. Instead, she stares at the opening of a tunnel.

Smiling, she throws another stone close to the wall on the left. Soon, the wall changes to another tunnel.

The final stone she holds on to for a moment. If the walls are tunnels, then what are the tunnels directly in front of her? She steps a couple feet into the room and the floor quakes under boots. She glances down just as the section she's standing on cracks and crumbles. Alyx leaps to the side before the section of floor breaks, disappearing into a black abyss below.

Breathing in snippets of air, she looks at Em and Crane. Em appears to be on the verge of a heart attack, or something. Crane shakes his head at her. Not to say she's stupid, but to not go any farther. At least that's how she reads it anyway. Maybe he does think she's stupid. Or crazy. Hell, he wouldn't be the first to think so.

The floor is made up of square sections, she quickly notes. They're about three feet wide, or so. Give or take. The question is: Which ones are rigged to break? The other thing is the edges are difficult to make out. There's too much dust covering the floor.

She sighs, and tosses the last stone. It lands, clicking along the floor, coming to a rest near the center of the large circle where it begins shifting through colors. Before it can reach pink, the stone begins to sink. Bubbles burst over the surface of the floor inside the circle. Then the stone vanishes under the floor.

"What the hell?" Crane bursts out.

Alyx, breaking out of her reverie, glances at the two men. "Just stay there."

Using the toe of her boot, she tests the nearest square. She presses harder and the square holds. Wiping sweat off her face with her hand, she adjusts her backward hat, and steps fully onto the square, eyes pinched shut. When the floor doesn't give way, Alyx blows out a long breath, too heavy to be a sigh and opens her eyes. The left tunnel is maybe ten squares away. Once hidden under some glamour or another, now revealed. It's the left tunnel they need to take, according to the map, but...

As she checks the next square, something in the room clinks. The sound bounces off the hewn stone walls like a ping-pong ball. She stops, trying to see everything at once. The silver circle rises out of the floor and begins to turn. Dust plumes as the raised circle clicks counter-clockwise.

Alyx blinks, cuts her sight to Em and Crane. "You two better move."

The men exchange a worried glance, and carefully make their way to her, stepping on the same squares.

The silver circle clicks, filling the room with dust. Inside the circle, the floor boils. Nothing in any of the texts she's read said anything about a boiling floor, or the turning circle, for that matter. That's why Morris is kind of important to this exploration. But he's gone now, and it's up to her to figure out what the hell to do.

From the fake tunnels to her right, a low groaning sound mingles with the clicks. A foul stench fills her nostrils. Something like rotting meat.

"Dr. Wick?" Em steps into her square. Way too close. The guy needs a damn shower.

"What?"

"You think maybe we should get to that tunnel before something bad happens?"

She grunts, claps him on the shoulder. "What would I do without you, Em?"

"Find some other fool to drag along with you on these crazyass explorations of yours," Crane spouted in his deep, rumbling voice.

Alyx chuckles, nods and turns to the tunnel.

"Wait, really?" Em, he's so close he's almost pushing her off the square now.

Alyx grins. "Gotta keep you on your toes." Then she jumps across the remaining squares to the mouth of the tunnel.

The moment her boots land in the tunnel, the clicking increases. The raised circle turns faster.

"Hurry," she tells Em and Crane.

Em jumps, but, being shorter, lands on the square directly in front of the tunnel. The floor cracks, crumbles. Alyx grabs the front of his jacket and yanks him into the tunnel with her. He's breathing too heavily to say much of anything and sort of collapses against the wall. Crane makes the jump without any problems.

The groaning gets louder. A shadow catches Alyx's sight from the tunnel across the room. She squints, trying to make it out. A ratcheting noise joins in with the clicks and groans. Then, in the gloom of the tunnel across the room, something metal gleams.

"*Go*," she shouts, pushing Em and Crane away from the opening. "Run!"

The two men ask no questions. They don't hesitate. They know her well enough that when she says run, it really means haul ass.

Alyx risks a glance over her shoulder just as there's a whoosh sound and two metal spikes stab into the stone wall inches from her head.

She stares, wide-eyed at the spikes still vibrating in the stone and says, "Traps. Why are there always traps?" Out of the corner of her eye, the gleam of metal in the dark.

Without further hesitation, Alyx sprints down the tunnel and around a slight curve to join Em and Crane. Behind her, the raised circle continues to click.

"You said there wouldn't be any crazy traps on this one," Em says, all bug-eyed.

Bringing out the map, Alyx says, "I said there *might* not be. Small difference."

"Small? I about *died* back there."

Alyx smiles. "But you didn't."

"How far are we to the Sythilias?" Crane asks, apparently not in the mood for bickering.

Alyx eyes the map. "Not far."

"Any more rooms that aren't rooms that try to kill people?" Em frowns at her.

She holds the map up for him to see. "Does it look like there are?"

He rolls his eyes and points his lights down the tunnel. "There's one thing I've learned going on explorations with you, Dr. Wick." He glances at her. "Maps don't mean shit."

This time, however, the map is right. There aren't any more rooms. No more traps. And if there are more of those creatures that tried to kill them earlier…there's no sign.

The air in the tunnel is cool on Alyx's sweaty skin. It's almost a relief. Up until now, the tunnels have been a balmy ninety degrees. Checking the thermal meter fixed to her wrist, it's currently sixty-four.

A couple turns finds them at their destination.

The tunnel yawns open, revealing a dark cavern. Here they linger.

"Set up the tall boys," Alyx says.

Em and Crane unpack the two stands fixed to wide, rectangular lamps. She steps back, letting them set the lamps up. They're maximum exposure, high density. But that's not what makes them so special. Their light spreads out in massive fans, making most of the insides of deep caverns visible.

Just a couple of the many toys she stole from the University before they kicked her out.

The men switch on the tall boy lamps and instantly the cavern is lit. It isn't as deep as she first thought and the lamps make it appear as daylight. Clear, every detail illuminated.

Through the texts and stories told by elders, the Sythilias is surrounded by giant serpents that guard the precious idol. It's said whoever tries to take the Sythilias from its alter shall die many deaths. It's said there are dark spirits who will enter you and force your body into convulsions, twisting your insides until there's nothing but pulp. All are fickle warnings. Pretty much the same kind of warnings she's debunked over the years. The only other warning that stands out, though, is by touching the Sythilias itself.

Legend has it, the Sythilias contains the very essence of a god. A god gone dormant, asleep until his time to wake arises. The god's name is, Reque. The Xyeth God of Death. And, as legend goes, he wasn't an evil god. Perhaps, he was even kind. For he took those who needed taking and if merely injured, he healed until that person's time to truly die arrived. Or something like that.

So, it is said, if one touches the skull idol for which Reque slumbers, the god will be transferred from the idol into the person, becoming a new vessel. A mobile idol. That person will be possessed by a god.

Of course, that's also just a story. Common legend through the Xyeth culture, which is all but extinct now. Morris is but one out of four hundred still alive today. And the bastard ran off on her.

"Dr. Wick, you seeing this?"

"Yeah, Em."

The cavern isn't large, but its ceiling is high. All of it appears to be chiseled out of black rock. Something like onyx, perhaps, only not as shiny. No, it's more like looking at charcoal. Glowing on its altar is the Sythilias. A misshapen blue skull. No one, not even the Xyethians themselves, know where the Sythilias came from.

Just one day, it appeared on the ground and, as told in many stories, the only one allowed to touch it was a Xyeth child by the name of Ruw. This child, she'd become the caretaker of the Sythilias. Its carrier during worship, and its guardian. For, whomever else tried to touch the blue skull would die. Their skin sloughed off. Their bones broke. Their bodies melted into slimy goop. Some later stories also contributed the near extinction of the Xyeth species to the Sythilias, and Ruw herself the bringer of plagues. Like the mummies of old on Earth. And once the devastation and near annihilation of the Xyethians was over, it's said the Sythilias sucked Ruw inside it, trapping her for eternity.

The history of it dates back to about the time dinosaurs roamed Earth. So…a very damn long time ago. Making this planet, Wumon, far older than Earth could ever dream to be. Earth, now barely a living thing as it lurches through the Milky Way.

Close to Alyx's ear, Crane says, "What's this thing worth?"

She smiles, "Enough for us all to retire."

Behind her, he says, "Bout time, lady."

Alyx chuckles, but her sight still scans the cavern. Nothing in the texts, or Morris's vague stories, told of any traps surrounding the Sythilias. And yet...there wasn't supposed to be traps in the Room of Tangles either.

There's always a trap.

"So," Em says. "What now?"

"Wait here," she says, gaze falling to the floor as she steps into the cavern. Her shadow is a giant against the far wall.

"Ten-four, Boss," Em spouts.

Alyx, shaking her head, stops to take another look around. The scent of something like fresh fruit drifts to her nostrils. A good smell. An inviting smell. A smell that gives her pause. The Sythilias is a sacred artifact. The Xyeths wouldn't want anyone trying to steal it. And through her experience, a good, inviting smell often means something worse than if there's a bad smell. A slight chill in the air crawls over her face and the back of her neck. Like a breath from an ice dragon, perhaps.

But, if there are traps here, they're hidden very well. She can't spot a single sign. Nothing even remotely out of place. Still, she wishes she had the stones to make sure what she's seeing is real and not just another glamour. The stones she left in the Room of Tangles for their return.

Stepping carefully, Alyx walks to the altar and stares at the Sythilias. It glows bright blue. A faint hum trembles the air. She looks over the altar itself, checking for any inconsistencies in the stone holding the Sythilias. Nothing. Just an old altar carved out of gray rock. A breath of relief spills out of her and she reaches for the Sythilias.

Very faint, a chattering sound rises.

Alyx pauses inches from the Xyeth artifact, eyes drifting back and forth in their sockets. Her heart quickens. Traps...

Slowly, she draws her hand away from the Sythilias. All her nerves spark at once. And yet...nothing happens. The chattering sound fades away. Laughing lightly to herself, she shakes her head, and picks the Sythilias up off the altar. Nothing happens. Sometimes nothing ever does with such explorations, though none as big as this one. The Sythilias will sell to the right galactic museum for all three of them to live well for the rest of their lives. This is it. This is her retirement. And at thirty-four, that's alright with her. Early retirement is a thing of beauty. No matter how much one enjoys the work, as she does, not having to worry about anything would be a proverbial heaven.

There was a time when she worked for the sheer joy of it. Finding the unfindable and delivering rare artifacts to various museums throughout the galaxies and—

A loud ratcheting noise crashes through her thoughts.

Somewhere behind her, Em says, "Oh shit."

The altar shakes, pieces of it crumbling away, and slowly, it begins to descend into the floor. Above, there's a peculiar crackling sound. A whiff of something burning finds her. Alyx backs away from the altar, cradling the Sythilias. Rocks fall from the ceiling of the cavern, shattering the remains of the altar.

"Um, Dr. Wick…you might wanna hurry." Em, sounding more than a little terrified.

The floor quakes under her, something makes a loud hiss. The burning odor grows more pungent. A sulfuric stench. The smell of…

A bright, glowing liquid splatters onto the ruined altar, instantly hissing and popping. A fiery crackle. Tiny sparks fly. She doesn't need to feel the heat to know what that liquid is.

Alyx spins, runs toward Em and Crane. "Go!"

Behind her, more lava falls from the ceiling. Just before she reaches the mouth of the tunnel, she risks a glance behind her. The ceiling breaks out and a giant lavafall crashes to the floor.

Em and Crane are already gone. She sprints into the tunnel, running as fast as her legs will carry her. The stone floor shudders. Behind her, the rush of lava. The heat builds, shoving into her back. The tunnel is a massive roar greater than any monster. A radiant, red glow lights her way. Ahead, she thinks she hears someone scream.

Coming to a stop at the edge of the Room of Tangles, floor shaking, heat blasting at her, she finds Crane clinging to the side of a solid square. His teeth are clenched and sweat sheens his broad forehead. Em, rummaging through one of the packs, keeps telling the large man to, "Just hold on, buddy. I got you. Just don't let go."

Alyx jumps onto the solid square beside Em. The man glances at her, then returns to fumbling through his pack.

"My fault," Em says over and over to himself. Even with the roar of the lava, Alyx hears him.

She smacks his arm and places the Sythilias on the next solid square. "We'll pull him up together."

Em blinks at her, almost appears dubious about the suggestion, then nods. He drops the pack and joins her near the edge where Crane still clings. His arms tremble.

He latches onto Alyx's hand, and shit, the guy is heavy. His weight pulls her closer to the edge.

"Em," she grunts. "His other hand."

But when she looks, he's jumping to the main tunnel and soon disappears.

Mostly through his teeth, Crane manages, "Took the Sythilias."

Alyx, eyes widening, quickly snatching a glance behind her at the square she placed the artifact on. Gone.

"That double crossing son of a bitch," she says and returns her attention to Crane.

"The asshole pushed me," the big man says.

He says something else, but the roaring of approaching lava is too great to hear him.

"What?"

He shakes his head.

The fiery glow intensifies near the mouth of the tunnel. A couple metal spikes fly over her head and stab into the wall, meeting with several others. She wishes one of those would have gotten Em, the traitor.

She grabs Crane's other arm, begins sliding closer to the edge. No matter how much she pulls and digs her heels in, the man is just too heavy. She needs to think of a way to counter balance the weight. Leverage…

Yet, as she scans the room, there's nothing. Maybe rope in the pack Em dropped, but if she lets go, Crane will surely fall. The heat in the room is becoming a menace. Sweat slithers down her face, and her grip on Crane turns slippery. He tries to pull himself up using her, but in doing so yanks her forward. Her right foot shoots out over the edge. Dust and small rocks fly, then plummet to whatever dark abyss awaits.

Teeth gritting, arms shaking, Alyx shouts, "Can you get a foothold on anything?"

Crane shakes his head. "Nothing there, and the pillar under you is too far. I'll pull you down with me."

"Shit," she manages, feeling her sweat slicked hands slip in his.

The first sight of molten rock rolls to the edge of the tunnel. She glares at it, then looks at Crane, tears filling her eyes.

In his deep, rumbling voice, Crane says, "Let go, Alyx."

"*What*? No, way. I can't—"

"Yes, you can. Thank you for all the great adventures, Dr. Wick. You're the best." His hands loosen.

She goes to readjust her hands, but everything is sheened in sweat. He slips right out of her grip and disappears into the darkness below.

"*No*," she cries, backing away from the edge of her square. She wipes tears from her face, glances at the lava spreading into the room. Some of it spills down the broken square she saved Em from falling in.

Should've let the asshole fall, she thinks.

Alyx grabs the pack, works her way to the main tunnel and runs to catch up with Em. That is…if she isn't already too late.

She jumps over the dead creature as everything around her cracks and quakes. The entire place is going to cave in. Heart hammering, Alyx pushes herself to run faster. Large chunks of stone crash behind her. The right side of the tunnel splits open, expelling a yellowish gas. She holds her breath, sprints through it and finally emerges outside. She makes it about fifty yards away, before the tunnel collapses, jetting acrid dust and sharp rocks at her back.

Breathing heavily, side aching from all the running, she drops to her knees, trying to catch her breath.

And the cold muzzle of a gun presses against her left temple.

"Glad you could join us, Dr. Wick."

She frowns. That slightly arrogant, nasally, heavily accented voice. She recognizes it. But it's been years since…

"Perhaps you should've learned by now. What's yours is mine in the end, eh?"

Her eyes shut, then open. "The Sythilias belongs in a museum, Vilas, you jackass."

Vilas, with his pompous chuckle, steps into view. An old, clean shaven white man with bushy gray eyebrows and a grin to rival the deadliest of snakes. "Come now, Dr. Wick. Sharing is caring. You of all people should know this."

Gun still pressed against her temple she says, "Is that so?"

"Yes," Em says to her left, confirming her thought of who might be behind the gun. Doesn't surprise her much.

"Oh, Em," she says. "You'll get yours soon enough."

"Dear Em, here," Vilas says, "will get half of what the Sythilias brings. More than you were going to give." He kneels in front of Alyx, grinning. "Perhaps you should hire more faithful assistants, eh?"

Alyx smiles, chuckles. "Perhaps you shouldn't underestimate me so much."

She drops, spins, and kicks the gun out of Em's hand. It lands in the dirt. He howls, going for the gun. She kicks again, stroking his twig and berries. Em, a thin whine issuing from his gaping mouth, collapses holding his groin.

Alyx is on her feet in an instant as Vilas, wide-eyed, backs away.

"Where is it?" she asks, keeping her tone mild. She's pissed beyond belief, but Vilas already knows that. He'll exploit it more if she reveals it too much.

"Safe," the wretched man says, grinning once more. "In my possession."

She draws her revolver and points it at Vilas. "You have till the count of five to hand the Sythilias over."

"Do you not realize whom you're speaking to, Dr. Wick?"

"Yup," she says. "An Earthling with a chip on his shoulder that should've died during the rampant plagues of Earth. And yet…here you are. One. Two…"

"You won't shoot me," Vilas spouts. "You're not a killer."

Alyx smirks, leveling the gun on his head. "Wanna try me? Three. Fou—"

A bunch of clicks stops her. In this moment, she realizes it's not just Vilas, Em and her, but…

Surrounding her are more than a few Xyethians, including Morris, whom points a gun of his own at her.

A long breath blows out her and she lowers the revolver.

Vilas, the arrogant bastard, he laughs. "You lose, Dr. Wick."

Holstering her gun, Alyx says, "Well, someone has to."

Vilas laughs, nods. "Yes, Dr. Wick, but sadly, I must give this meeting a close. I'm a very busy man, you see and have much to do." Not far behind him is a cruise ship. A very luxurious one.

"I bet," Alyx says.

Vilas winks, nods to the Xyeths, and walks toward his awaiting ship.

Morris and the others close in, guns pointing at Alyx. Em steps in front, blocking her view of Vilas. His face is all red, eyes the very definition of pissed off.

"Hey, Em," she says, nods toward his groin. "How's the cluster?"

He blinks, points his gun at her. "You never respected me."

"You know, I kind of did. Well, until you murdered your friend and turned traitor, of course. Up until that moment, though, I had a lot of respect for you."

"Bullshit," he shouts. "You never listened to anything I said. Treated me like a servant."

"You were my *assistant*, jackass."

"Jus'shoot'er already," Morris says. "Gotta go meet Vilas and get paid."

Alyx laughs. She can't help it. "You guys really think he's going to pay you?"

13

Em straightened. "We signed contracts. He has to."

Again, she laughs, this time louder. When it eases, she says, "Oh, is that right? Well, then, you best get moving."

Em, smiling a bit, says, "Part of the contract is killing you."

"Aww, isn't that just a kick in the nuts?" She grins.

Em visibly cringes, and says, "Good-bye, Dr. Wick."

Alyx draws her revolver, lightning quick, shoots off Em's gun hand, drops to a knee and takes out all ten of the Xyeths. Em, screaming, staring at the bleeding stump where his hand used to be, staggers away.

Vilas is just now about to board his ship. He doesn't look back.

Alyx aims the gun at his back. Releases a slow breath, and pulls the trigger.

Vilas stumbles, falls.

She wastes no time and runs toward Vilas's ship. She needs to get the Sythilias back and get the hell off this planet.

Dirt sprays up a few feet in front of her. She stops. Another spray of dirt catches her. The ground under her vibrates. Somewhere in the distance, something squeals. Most of the Xyethians are gone, very true, but the animals of the planet are still very much alive. Still very hungry.

Alyx swallows down a lump in her throat, starts toward Vilas once more. A long, toothy snout bursts out of the dirt, snaps shut inches from her. She skids to a stop, spins and runs away from it. The ground rolls, as if made of liquid, rather than dirt. Keeping her balance is a task unto itself. Yet, she manages and hurries toward her ship, the Starry Night. Everything is coming to life around her. Trees tilting and whispering. Creatures crawling, slithering, stalking closer and closer. All of the excitement must have caught their attention.

As she approaches the rear hatch it opens, sensing her presence. An update Crane installed before this exploration. Poor Crane, faithful till the very end. Tears threatened to blur her vision, but she fought them back. No time to grieve now.

Through the trees, something crashes. The ground moves, yet remains solid. The monsters of Wumon were waking up to feed. And what's better than food, than new food, right?

Alyx boards the Starry Night, shuts the rear hatch and makes her way to the bridge where all the controls are. She straps into her chair, hits the bottom thruster boosters, and slowly pulls the lever back. The small ship rises off the ground. She lifts the legs, pulls the lever back farther and she's now above the trees. The image screen reveals a sight that forces a shiver out of her.

All kinds of creatures watch from the spot where she lifted off. Monsters to many who don't know Wumon's various species. Things with sharp teeth, long claws, and narrow glowing eyes. Things that'll eat you up.

She sighs, touches the engine pad, taps her destination—Planet Quins—and sets the ship to rapid drive.

Alyx leans back, tears once more filling her eyes for her fallen assistant and friend.

She thinks about Crane. Thinks about Em. And wants to punch Vilas in his smug, wrinkly face.

"I'll find you, Vilas," she says to herself. "Then you'll wish you hung around to kill me yourself."

Then again, she shot him. If he's not dead, then he's hurt bad. Once out of Wumon's atmosphere she does a scan of the area she left. There's nothing there. Nothing besides the monsters. The real monster, however, is gone.

Alyx Wick shuts her eyes as her ship shoots off toward Planet Quins.

Tomorrow is Monday, and life goes on.

TWO

"So," Alyx says, stepping away from her desk and clasping her hands in front of her. "Can anyone tell me the most important thing to consider before entering a tomb on the planet Verna?"

The kids, all early twenty somethings, they smile. Well, most of them. There's a few in the back playing with their pads and ignoring everything. About ten raise their hands.

She nods at a thin boy sitting in the front row. "Cullin."

Cullin, he stands up, rubs his palms on his pink pants and chuckles nervously. His narrow face twitches in its usual tick. His dark eyes shift back and forth. He must've forgotten to comb his thick shock of brown hair this morning, because it's a twisted mess today. He doesn't need to stand, but Cullin likes to be heard, she knows. Despite him not being very smart.

"Um, be aware of traps?"

Alyx smiles, nods and half turns away from the boy. "Good. But what's the very first rule before entering?"

"I-Um...scanning, maybe?"

Still smiling, Alyx goes to the board, a large clear plastic thing. She picks up the pen, and as she writes, the words glow on the board. This huge thing that replaced white boards and black boards centuries ago. All digital. She scribbles on the board, words lighting up as she goes.

"Can you tell me what this passage is from, Cullin?"

She finishes writing: One must, first and foremost, cleanse your spirit before desecration of ruins.

She looks at Cullin, this frightfully thin boy in pink pants and untamed hair. The boy's eyes shift away in thought. Around him, a few of the other students raise their hands. Yes, they know, but she wants Cullin to get it. She wants to see him shine.

Then, finally, his eyes widen. He smiles and looks at her. "It's from famed explorer, Melvin Rouse's book."

Alyx wants to hug the kid. "Very good, Cullin. Yes, Melvin Rouse, the first human intergalactic explorer. The very first to explore our planet." She rounds her desk and nods to Cullin. "Can you tell me what he means with this passage?"

Still smiling a little, Cullin says, "He doesn't mean cleanse your soul, but your mind. So you can...um...think outside the box. To have an open mind?"

Chuckling, Alyx nods, and says, "Yes. That exactly, Cullin. Very well done. You may sit now."

Beaming, face lit up in triumph, the boy sits. It's this look Alyx is addicted to. That ah-ha, moment when all the lights turn on. When a student finally gets it and understands. As a professor, this is what she strives for. And she's happy to see it on Cullin's face right now. The boy isn't the smartest, but he tries, and that's what matters.

The other students blink at him for a moment, then give her their attention again. The girl next to him smiles, reaches over and places a hand on his. He visibly flinches, caught off guard, but then relaxes and smiles back at her. Amy. Of course it's Amy. Those two are like peas in a pod.

Now, Alyx passes a hand over the board, erasing the Rouse passage.

"Your assignment this week," she says to the class, writing on the board, "is to read page five-hundred and twenty in Rouse's book, The Divine and The Hidden. I want you to explore something. Anything. There are caves. Go inside, look around. By the end of the week, I want you to bring me what you found during your explorations."

"Dr. Wick?"

She pauses, glances over her shoulder. It's a girl in the back, one of those who were on their pads through class.

"Yes, Emilia?"

"You want us to explore around here?"

Alyx turns. "No. I want you to explore *everywhere*. I want you to dig deep. Travel beyond city limits, though safely. I want you to open your minds to the possibilities."

Emilia shoots Alyx a thumbs up and returns her attention to the pad on her desk. The girl is one of the brightest in the class. Just a bit distant. Her mind turns at a different pace than others, that's all.

"Is this a test?" A boy on the far left asks.

Ah, Brady. A huge young man who'd rather be playing football than taking her class. Not very bright, but dedicated and manages a C average.

"No," Alyx says. "This is a real exploration, but I want you to follow the steps indicated on page five-hundred and twenty of Rouse's book. I want you all to also document everything. Video documentation, so I can watch your approach."

Brady rolls beady eyes, blows out a heavy breath, but nods.

Alyx opens her mouth for further instruction when the end of class buzzer brays. The class stands, grabbing their pads.

As they swarm toward the door, Alyx shouts over the commotion. "Remember to read the page before exploring. Video document your discoveries and above all, have fun!"

She's not sure if anyone heard her, but such is the life of a professor at the end of class.

Sometime later, she's locking her classroom door behind her and walking to her office when a frightfully tall woman falls in stride beside her.

"Dr. Alyx Wick?"

Alyx snorts. "Maybe. And you are?"

"Dr. Wick, it's a pleasure to meet you finally. I'm General Hunt of the A-9 Marines."

"General Hunt," Alyx says, eyes focusing on her office door at the end of the hall. Her refuge. "Ten time galactic war decorated. Six stars. You led the A-9 into the Battle of Fallow to end the Gow War."

"Yes. The very same."

"What can I help you with, General Hunt?"

"You came very highly recommended by a colleague of yours. A Mr. Sullivan White."

"Ah, Sully." Alyx smiles with all the memories of her earlier exploration with her good friend. "How's that old coot doing these days?"

"Well, Dr. Wick, we're not sure."

Frowning, Alyx stops and turns to the tall woman, this A-9 Marine General. "What do you mean?"

Hunt sighs. "Dr. Wick, Mr. White went missing three days ago."

Alyx blinks, all the air whooshing out of her lungs at once, as if she's been kicked in the stomach. "W-what happened?"

General Hunt's gaunt face slackens. Her eyes soften. "Do you have an office?"

THREE

Sitting on the other side of Alyx's cluttered desk, General Hunt sighs heavily. She glances around the small office.

"Cozy," the General says.

"More like contained chaos," Alyx says. "Are you going to tell me about Sully or critique my office, General Hunt?"

Hunt smiles the tiniest bit, yet her eyes become flinty. Hard and cold. Alyx can tell she's the type not used to taking orders. Ever. Or being questioned, for that matter.

And yet, Hunt leans back in the chair. It creaks a bit from her weight. This giant of a woman with her short, brunette hair and piercing, bright green eyes. Another sigh flows out of the General.

"Mr. White was on assignment for us to explore and evaluate an unknown planet in the Wood Wyrm Galaxy. He—"

"Wood Wyrm? That's a hostile galaxy. Why would you send him there?" Alyx bites back on her anger. The military could be real assholes sometimes. Dipping their clumsy fingers in where they don't belong.

Hunt shrugs. "There's a certain planet we are interested in there. One void of life, yet is fully sustainable. Ten times larger than our old Earth, and clean. Fresh. We can recolonize. A better future for our species than remaining here on Quins, which will soon be overpopulated."

"So," Alyx says. "You want to basically take over another planet and destroy it too?"

Hunt's face is stony. "No, Dr. Wick. Our scientists have come up with advanced eco-circulators that will stop any and all pollution." She leans forward a bit. "Dr. Wick, we have a real chance to relocate to a planet where the human race can finally thrive once more."

Alyx waves a dismissive hand. She's heard this before from other officials. Once, Quins was supposed to be the savior of the human race. Now it's grossly overcrowded and becoming a polluted cesspool like old Earth. Humans, Alyx has come to the conclusion, are filthy creatures.

"Anyway, what happened to Sully?"

General Hunt shrugs. "This, we're not sure of. The exploration was well underway, Mr. White documenting everything as he went. Then, all communications were lost. He had six Marines with him, Dr. Wick. Six of my elite. None of them are responsive."

Alyx's heart quickens. "But it's only been three days, maybe there's a solar flare interrupting the coms?"

"No solar flares. No disturbances of any kind were detected. One second communication was ongoing, the next, they all vanished. Our scans find no lifeforms."

"So you think they're all dead?"

Hunt shakes her head. "We believe they may have fallen into a precipice. Perhaps they're injured, but more than likely there's a certain graphite in the stone blocking the coms."

Alyx's sight drifts to an old picture sitting on her desk. One of her and Sully after they discovered the Wylium. A powerful crystal that can produce enough energy to power an entire small planet for five hundred years. She smiles a bit, remembering how happy they were that day Sully spotted the sparkling tip of the crystal hidden in the tomb of an unknown alien race. It had been the discovery of the decade, the Wylium able to give sustainable power to Quins.

Back when times were easier and money not an issue. Back when she had real friends.

She kept in touch with Sully over the years, but as their schedules drifted in opposite directions, they fell out of communication with each other. He went on to be renowned, while she became sort of infamous. She gave her findings to museums, but only if they paid. He just gave and asked for nothing in return. Exploration, for Sully White, had always been about the discovery, not the pay off. Without him, without his nobility and honor, Alyx found herself feeling like a pirate.

"Dr. Wick," General Hunt says, slicing through Alyx's memories. "We'd like you to go find Mr. White and the missing Marines."

Alyx lifts an eyebrow at Hunt. "You can't go there yourselves? I'm sure you have plenty of amazing trackers."

Hunt nods. "We do. But, this is a covert operation. The Government doesn't know about it yet, and we'd like to keep it that way. More manpower will require asking for more funds. We can't let that happen."

"So…the military are pulling a fast one on the Government, huh?" She snorts, leans back in her chair. "Oh, you're gonna be in a lot of trouble when the Big Guys figure out what's going on behind their backs."

For the first time, General Hunt, her in her black pantsuit and gimlet gaze, appears angry. She straightens in her chair. "We'll reveal our discovery in due time, Dr. Wick. If V-10 is as hospitable as our scans show, we'll be saving the human race from extinction."

"Will you now…" Alyx stands, turns to a shelf of ancient texts. "What's in it for me? Besides finding my dear friend. What are you offering?"

"Dr. Wick." Hunt stands, starts to round the desk, then stops. "Your career as an explorer is…less than pristine, unlike that of the professor here. I might even venture to call you a thief and a space pirate. But you are the only one who can do what I ask. Find Mr. White and my six Marines."

"And that's all? You just send me to this V-10 planet and I go find Sully and your kids? No catch?"

Hunt smiles. "No catch."

Turning back to the texts, Alyx says, "You never answered what you're offering me in exchange."

"You will be rewarded, Dr. Wick. Handsomely. And your less than savoy career as an explorer will be expunged."

"How handsomely?"

Behind her, Hunt is quiet for a moment, then says, "Enough to where you'll be working here for free, if you so choose."

Alyx faces the General. "You're saying I can retire?"

Hunt, smiling, nods. "And live out the rest of your life in comfort."

Alyx sighs, sight falling on the picture of her and Sully once more. "Deal."

"Very well," General Hunt says, walking toward the door. "I'll have a vehicle waiting for you outside." She opens the door.

"When do you need me?"

Hunt, over her shoulder. "Now." The tall woman shuts the door behind her, leaving Alyx alone in her office. She stares at the picture of her and Sully for a few minutes, gathers up her things, and walks to the Dean's Office.

Dean Helena sits behind her massive crystal desk swatting flies and murmuring her disgust.

Alyx leans in the doorway, smiling, arms crossed over her chest until Helena notices her.

"Oh, Allie! Come in, come in." She slaps a plastic flyswatter down, completely missing a fat black fly. "You know, the one thing we could've left behind on that wretched Earth were the flies. But, oh-no, not us. We needed to bring them with, didn't we? Stupid, ugly things." *Slap*. And another miss.

Alyx chuckles, sits across from Helena. Most of the exploration assignments, they come from Helena. Going back almost fifteen years, they've not only cultivated a great work relationship, but a strong friendship as well. And in a Universe where nothing is certain, friendship is a rare thing to come by.

"So," Helena says, smacking at another fly and missing. "Who do I owe the pleasure of this unscheduled meeting?"

"Remember Sully White?"

Helena blinks. "Why, of course. How is he?"

Alyx sighs. "He's missing. On a planet in the Wood Wyrm Galaxy."

Helena drops her flyswatter, eyes wide. "*What*? That galaxy is…why was he *there*?"

"He was working for the military. They found a large planet there, resembling Earth. The military hired him to check the place out."

The older woman across from Alyx shakes her head. "Oh, this is awful. Simply awful. Sully is such a good man. Such a great explorer."

"Yes," Alyx says and leans forward a bit. "I was just hired today to go find him."

"You…wait, *what*?"

Alyx nods. "I leave right away. Can you get Kyle Reamus to sub in for my class? I'll leave notes, of course."

Fidgeting a bit, Helena says, "I can, indeed. But, Allie, this sounds like suicide. No telling what's on that planet, and the military is a fickle beast to work with."

Alyx winks. "Wouldn't be the first time I went into the unknown."

"Well, yes, but this…Allie, it feels wrong."

"They're offering me retirement," Alyx says.

Helena's steely eyebrows lift a little. "Retirement? Allie, honey, you're barely thirty-five."

"Exactly. I can relax for the rest of my life."

Helena laughs the tiniest bit. "Allie, I've known you for sixteen years and never known you to relax."

Alyx shrugs. "Maybe I'll do some travelling."

The Dean of the University of Quins simply chuckles, shakes her head and says, "This is insane, Allie. You know that correct?"

Grinning, Alyx says, "Of course."

Helena's face slackens a bit, her tone serious. "Are you absolutely sure about this?"

"Ha. No. But, when am I sure about anything, right?"

Helena, face solemn, nods slowly. "Correct." She leans forward. "You just make sure they give you a contract and that you sign it. Also, please do be sure you have a contingency plan."

"Yes, Mom."

"Allie." Helena reaches across her desk to grip Alyx's hands in hers. "Be careful with this one, okay? Be wary."

Alyx smiles, but inside, her heart thunks. Helena, always the mother hen, never gets so serious. Nor has she ever been so against a job as she is with this one. It gives Alyx pause and she begins questioning her decision making skills. Which is also new. She tries to never overthink an exploration, or in this case, a rescue mission. Doesn't matter, she never overthinks. Never second guesses when it pertains to an exploration. She reserves that for the professor gig.

"Promise me, Allie," Helena says. "Promise me you will be wary."

She sighs. "Yes. Okay. I will, Helena." She stands as Helena rounds the desk and wraps her arms around her. The hug is firm, full of love. And when they part, Helena kisses Alyx's cheek.

"Be safe, Allie."

Alyx smiles, nods and hurries out of the office before tears blur her vision.

FOUR

The vehicle waiting outside isn't black.

It's bright yellow. Too bright to be a taxi.

This throws her off a little. When she thinks of covert operations and military she thinks black, but apparently that's not the case here.

In a suitcase, she carries her gear. Lucky black leather jacket, ballcap, and revolver. The things she carries with her everywhere she goes.

As she approaches the bright yellow cruiser, a fat man in a replica Hawaiian shirt steps out of the driver's side and walks around the vehicle to meet her. His jowls jiggle with every step. His breathing is made up of harried gulps and wheezy exhales.

"Dr. Wick?" This man asks, in his fake loafers and tan cargo shorts and messy blond hair.

"Yup," she says, sighs. "This the cruiser to Hell?"

The man's beady eyes blink. "Huh?"

Alyx snorts, shakes her head. "Nothing."

"General Hunt hired me to shuttle you to Compound-A." He glances around before his eyes fall to the suitcase in her hand. "No other luggage?"

"Nope. This is all I need. Let's go."

"Right-O, Dr. Wick. Let's go." He jiggles back around to the driver's side.

Alyx chuckles lightly, shakes her head, and gets in the backseat of the cruiser. The seats are made of slippery leather-like material questionable in origin. Although Quins boasts cattle, they are regarded crucial only to food. Leather isn't a thing, unless it's replicated by material printers, much like the fat man's Hawaiian shirt. It smells a little like pickles in here.

"How long of a ride will it be?" she asks.

Touching the drive pad in front of his considerable gut, the man says, "Oh, 'bout twenty minutes. Compound-A is kinda secret, ya know?"

"Yeah," Alyx says. "Don't want protestors getting gunned down, now do we."

"What was that, Dr. Wick?" The big man, tapping away on his drive pad as the cruiser lifts off the street.

"I said, I know it is."

"Right, right," the big man says. "I'm Kevin, by the way."

"Well, nice to meet you, Kevin. Are we going to go anywhere or just kind of float here?"

"Oh, ayuh. This old thing takes a bit to get movin'. My apologies, Dr. Wick."

"Alyx, please."

"Alyx. Right, right. Okay, here we go."

The cruiser jolts forward and then, finally, they're on their way.

Alyx leans back, catching a snippet of sleep before arriving.

FIVE

Thirty minutes later, not twenty, Kevin lowers the cruiser to the ground in front of a dilapidated two-story house. Something one might see in Earth History Texts of Victorian style homes. She's seen enough pictures to know this much. But *this* house, it's so old. Like it's been standing here on this otherwise deserted street for hundreds of years.

A slumped, neglected thing. At one time, perhaps it was a painted white, but now the paint curls away from gray, weathered siding, filthy with time and neglect. The large front porch slouches to the right, the pillars holding the roof up over the porch slants severely. More than a few windows are broken, while the rest are dark, dead eyes staring at her.

"This is Compound-A?"

Kevin grunts. "If so, the military really needs help."

"You sure you got the address right?"

Opening the door, Kevin says, "Of course. I'm not an idiot."

He gets out, shuts the door, and Alyx mutters, "I think the jury is still out on that one, my friend."

She hauls herself out of the cruiser and frowns at the old house.

Huffing next to her, sweat beading on his sloping forehead, Kevin says, "Well, good luck, Dr. Wick."

"Hey, thanks, Kevin. You're my hero."

He shoots her a confused look, shakes his chubby head and hurries back to his cruiser. A moment later, he's gone.

She sighs, clears her throat and walks through the high weeds choking the front lawn. They whisper across her pants. Lost whispers no one can ever understand. There are no insects here. No grasshoppers. No butterflies. Not even one of Helena's fat black flies. There's nothing here but the rot of a misplaced house and the empty silence of nowhere.

This isn't Compound-A. It can't...

Then her sight snags on the tiniest glint of metal near the door. Not the knob, which is a tarnished, misshapen thing, but something...out of place. Something that shouldn't be amongst such a ruin.

The closer she gets to the porch, the more the object comes into view. It's partially hidden but there. A keypad?

About twenty feet from the porch, a loud voice booms. "Halt! State your name and business."

She stops, eyes shifting, trying to pick out inconsistencies. She can't find anything other than the partial keypad.

"Dr. Alyx Wick. General Hunt invited me."

Silence once more overwhelms everything.

Then a shrill beep sounds and the front door opens. Not with a creaking or groan, but with a sly swish.

"Proceed, Dr. Wick. General Hunt will meet you at the end of the hall."

She nods. "Thanks."

After a final glance around, she mounts the crooked steps, which are surprisingly solid, and steps through the doorway. The door swishes shut behind her, locks with an audible click that echoes through the narrow white hall she now stands in. Lights embedded in the ceiling gives her a clear view all the way down the hall. Or as far as she can see, anyway. It seems to never end. A shiny, white tube, is what it feels like. Too narrow. The walls brush her shoulders as she walks. There are no doors. Nothing but white. Her heart thumps heavily with every step. Tight spaces aren't typically an issue for her, but this…all the white. The way everything gleams in the no nonsense lights. There's just something so different here than any dangerous situation she's been tossed into. Something even more unknown.

Still, she continues on until she finally comes to the end of the hall.

General Hunt is nowhere to be seen.

She stands here, glancing around, not sure what the hell she's supposed to do now. About to give up and just start shouting for Hunt, a strong, woman's voice says, "Dr. Wick. I'm glad you made it."

Alyx turns and finds herself staring up at the tall General. Hunt smiles.

"We need to keep a low profile. I apologize for the confusion."

"You might want to cover that keypad better, then."

Hunt frowns, then her eyes brighten. "Oh, you mean the body heat sensor. Well, it needs to be partially uncovered to detect heat sigs."

Feeling a bit on the stupid side—of course it's a heat sensor, duh—Alyx chuckles. She points down the long, white hall. "What's with the creepy, narrow hall?"

"For any infiltrators." Hunt, hands clasped behind her back turns to the long hall. "This entire surface is lutarium based, conducts laser grids that will slice apart anything we do not allow to enter."

"Touché," Alyx says.

Moving away from the long hall, Hunt turns left, and Alyx follows. This hall they walk in, it's wider, and all steel. The lights are set along the walls. Not as bright as the long, white hall with laser cutters or whatever the hell Hunt meant.

They come to steel double doors. Hunt passed her wrist over a pad near the doors and they whisper open, sliding into the walls on either side. These open up to a small room.

General Hunt beckons for Alyx to follow. Once inside, the doors whisper shut again. Alyx takes in the small room. It's painted lime green, lined with all sorts of monitors. In front of the monitors are men and women tapping away on screens. None of them appear to notice the two women, or at least Alyx doesn't think so.

"This next room is the Clean Room. It sanitizes you and scans for any devices not allowed beyond this point. It also can detect implants. This is merely a safety precaution, you understand."

"Sure," Alyx says as another set of doors open.

"I'll meet you in the next room and from there we'll get on with the briefing."

"Fantastic," Alyx says, stepping into the Clean Room.

The doors shut, a small beep sounds, and suddenly she's sprayed with an acrid smelling liquid from every possible direction. She manages, just barely, to cover her eyes before the stuff gets in them. The liquid dries almost instantly. There's another series of beeps. A few flashes of light. Then a mild buzzer sounds. Across the room, doors slip open.

Shaking her head, Alyx hurries out of the Clean Room and into another small room. This one void of anything. Just an empty room. Standing near yet another set of doors is Hunt. She's smiling thinly.

"We'll go down a couple flights of stairs, then enter the Briefing Room. I want to thank you again, Dr. Wick, for accepting our offer."

Alyx shrugs. "As long as I get a contract to sign and agree to the terms, we're golden, General."

Hunt nods, passes her wrist over a sensor pad and the doors open. "Very good. Follow me, please."

The stairs are metal and Alyx notes slight creases in the walls where each step connects. Are these laser cutters too? Hard to tell, but considering all the craziness so far, Alyx wouldn't put it past these guys. Yes, the Military are a strange bunch, for sure. Over cautious, even. She understands security, but this…it seems to be too much. What are they hiding here?

Their footfalls echo through the stairwell. Hunt's heavy boots clomp, while Alyx's slightly lighter boots quietly thunk. The stairs feel like they go down forever, and there's a strange chemical smell in the air that churns Alyx's stomach a bit.

Finally, they reach the bottom and Hunt leads her down another short hall. This one is lined with offices, or at least what resemble offices. The doors are all opaque glass, hard to see through and she can't tell if there are people in the small rooms or not.

Hunt opens one of the doors and gestures for Alyx to go inside.

Alyx is greeted by a roomful of people sitting around a large, oval table. They all turn to look at her. She rolls her eyes and plops down in a seat next to a big man with a serious body odor problem. The one thing she hates more than most is being the center of attention. She works better on the outskirts. Watching, observing, taking mental notes. But, being who she is, she's typically stuck in the middle of the chaos. All eyes are on her, regardless.

"So, you must be the adventurer," a small woman with a gleaming, shaved head across the table spouts.

Alyx lifts an eyebrow. "Explorer."

The woman chuckles humorlessly, waves a hand at Alyx. "Same thing."

"Not really, but whatever tips your boat, lady."

The woman's oval face grows stony. Her eyes are cold flints of steel.

The big man next to Alyx grunts. "Ignore Gerty. She hasn't had her coffee yet."

The woman, Gerty, shoots a glare at the big man. "I would have if you hadn't rushed me, Rip."

Rip shrugs. "Briefing is at eighteen hundred."

Gerty slaps the table. "It's seventeen-forty right now, jackass."

"Can't be late to briefings, dear."

"All I wanted was a cup of coffee, man."

"Should we all leave you two alone?" Alyx flashes a smile at both of them.

The big man, Rip, grins, but Gerty is all rage. Her face turns dark red.

"Don't mind Gerty," Rip says, "she's a good girl."

"Up yours, Rip."

Alyx chuckles.

"Okay," General Hunt says as she makes her way toward the front of the room, ahead of the table. "We don't have much time."

A man near the head of the table, face twisted in scars, and spiky black hair, says, "Took ya long enough, General."

Hunt narrows her gaze on him. "This is a briefing, Captain Row, not a debate." She looks at the rest of the people at the table. "No one talks until the end. We have much to cover."

Captain Row sighs, shakes his head. His eyes find Alyx. They're white. No pupils. He stares at her for a long time, not moving. A shiver scuttles under her skin. And when he finally turns away to focus on Hunt, Alyx breathes a sigh of relief. Not many men can creep her out, but Captain Row did it.

It's then, as Hunt readies herself for the briefing, Alyx realizes almost everyone else in the room is a Marine. Soldiers. Warriors. She's the only explorer.

"As all of you know," General Hunt says in her loud voice, "Company 3 landed on a habitable planet in the Wood Wyrm Galaxy no more than three days ago. As you also know, we lost coms with our brothers and sisters there, along with renowned explorer, Sullivan White."

At the mention of Sully, Alyx straightens a little. He's the reason she's here in the first place. That and retirement, of course. But mostly, she wants to find her friend. He's too good to be lost. Her mind shuffles through all the memories with him. Nothing romantic, but something close to sibling love. A closeness lost over the years due to her selfishness. She chose the way of a semi-pirate, while he stuck on the righteous path. She regrets the decision most days, but retiring early has been a goal for a while. Something she can't let go of, no matter how much she tries to renew her wonder of the galaxies and what discoveries she might find.

"Three days isn't long," Hunt continues, "but Company 3 was instructed to keep communication regularly every hour, on the hour. For three days, they have all fallen silent. We did receive a strange string of communications the day they presumably disappeared." Hunt taps a pad on the wall and suddenly the room is filled with static.

Harried breathing sifts through the static. Then…

"Can't…I'm alone, Base. Base, request immediate evac. Anyone there? Ah Christ."

Static crackles through, then another voice leaks through.

"We need immediate evac, Base! Structures are—"

More static drowns out everything for a few moments. Before Alyx can sigh, however…

"…trapped. Dr. White to Base. We are trapped inside a—"

Static explodes, so loud Alyx has to clap her hands over her ears.

Hunt taps the pad and the static stops. She sighs heavily as her eyes float over them.

"They're trapped in something. We don't know what and topical scans of the New World show us little. For all we know they've fallen into a sink hole of some kind. But here's where you come in, Company 1. Your mission is to locate and assist Company 3 and Dr. White in the further exploration of New World."

The General steps away from the table a bit, nods.

Captain Row raises his hand.

"Row?"

He clears his throat, leans forward a bit, the side of his heavily scarred face twitching as he speaks. "Once found, we are only to assist? Why not return home?"

"Because, Captain Row, we don't know what threats are on the New World. The more protection Dr. White has, the better."

"And what exactly is this Dr. White trying to explore?" This from an older woman across from Row.

After a moment, Hunt blows out a breath and says, "There's a very special artifact said to be on that planet. Something that might possess the power to create...and destroy worlds."

"Ah," Gerty says. "The plot thickens."

"Ma'am," Rip says. "With all due respect, couldn't such an artifact be dangerous?"

Hunt smiles. "In the wrong hands, yes. But in ours, Rip...we could create our very own world. One large enough to sustain our race for thousands of years. Ten times better than Earth ever was. We can be our own gods."

"More like you'll be a god," Gerty mutters.

"What's that, Sergeant?"

Gerty shakes her head. "Nothing, General Hunt, Ma'am."

Alyx, glaring at the General, stands. "You lied to me."

Hunt's eyes drift to Alyx.

"You said that planet was sustainable for the human race. You said that's why Sully is there. To explore it. To make sure everything is good before colonizing. So, General Hunt, I suggest you start being straight with me from now on."

"Or what, Dr. Wick?" There's a glint of challenge in her eyes.

"Or *what*? Or I'm not going to help you. I'm not one of your lackeys here."

"Asshole," Gerty spouts.

Hunt chuckles softly, the humorless chuckle of a hungry animal, walks around the table toward Alyx. "Oh, Dr. Wick, you *will* help us. You *will* go to that planet."

"No," Alyx says. "Not like this. There's no contract signed, I'm not obligated."

That humorless chuckle shudders out of Hunt's mouth again. "Ah, now, what would Dr. White think? You staying behind. The only person on this ugly planet, this entire *galaxy*, who can find him, and you just walk away?" Hunt clucks, shaking her head. "Oh, that is cold, Dr. Wick." The woman towers over Alyx now.

All eyes are back on Alyx. She feels them, their heat. Their stabbing. Burns that go deep.

She straightens, never one to back down from anyone. "Sully would understand. He'd never want me to be involved in something like this."

Smirking, Hunt says, "But he did. He went in knowing full well what he needed to find for us."

"That was his choice. A shitty one, but his."

Hunt's blue eyes fix on Alyx's green ones. The chilly glare of a predator. "You have two options here, Dr. Wick. Either you go and find your friend and help with the search, or you don't, and...well..." The taller woman shrugs.

"What the hell is that supposed to mean?"

"You're a smart girl," General Hunt says. "You can figure it out."

Alyx's heart quickens. This isn't how she works. This isn't what was supposed to happen. "You're the Marines. Honorable. Not terrorists."

Leaning closer, inches from Alyx's face, Hunt says, "This is a mission to save our species from extinction. You call us terrorists one more time and you'll see what true pain feels like, Dr. Wick."

This isn't how the military is supposed to act. This isn't how things are supposed to be.

And yet, Alyx laughs. She can't help it. It just rolls out of her, wave after wave.

Still inches from her, General Hunt frowns. "I don't believe I said anything in the least humorous, Dr. Wick."

Trying to stow the laughter, and failing, Alyx manages, "I'm sorry, but...this is just so ridiculous."

"What, exactly, is ridiculous about this briefing, Dr. Wick?" There's a hint of venom in Hunt's tone.

Alyx, finally choking down the remaining chuckles, waves a hand at the Marines seated at the table. All of them share about the same expression. Wide-eyed, slack jawed. They probably know, if they talked to Hunt like this they'd already be on their way to whatever fate awaited them.

So, this is the new military? A bunch of thugs, basically? Or, maybe, she's just not understanding what's really going on here.

"Okay," Alyx says, staring Hunt in the eyes. "So, if I don't help you then you hurt me? Is this how it works?"

There's a few seconds of silence. Long enough for Alyx to ready herself for escape if she has to. Laser hall be damned.

But Hunt only smiles and directs her attention to the front of the room. "No one said you'll be hurt one way or the other, Dr. Wick, but, if I may show you some history about the planet you'll be travelling to."

The lights in the room dim. On the large, white wall, a black planet streamed with green and blue pops into view.

Hunt steps beside the image. "As I'm sure you're all aware, this is our New World. This is where you'll be deployed."

Alyx sighs and leans against the far wall, hating herself for signing up on a fool's mission.

"And as I've mentioned, very little is known about New World. What we do know is that most of it is dead, or dormant."

Someone, Alyx isn't sure who, spouts, "More like a fucking dead world. This is bullshit."

Hunt continues as though no one had spoken at all. "When I say dead or dormant, I mean intelligent life. The planet appears, in every sense of the word, alive. There are animals and plants, and for these reasons I'd like to caution you before your arrival. Before you even set foot on New World, we did receive communication from Company 3 about the wildlife there." The image on the wall goes dark. The lights brighten and Hunt steps front and center again. "It's a hostile environment, folks. Brutal. Stay alert at all times and watch each other's backs. And I don't give a shit if you hate each other. This mission is fully funded and losing one of you would cost us more than you can imagine." Hunt's gaze flickers to Alyx, then away. "Despite this, however, despite the money involved, you are humanity's last hope. And humans stick together. We fight. We watch out for each other." She slams a fist on the table between Row and the older woman, startling both of them. "We *care* about each other."

After a moment of silence, Gerty says, "Great speech, General. So true. But what happens if we get into trouble? Any backup procedure in place in case, say…oh I dunno, we end up like fucking Company 3?"

"You're addressing a superior officer, Corporal," Hunt says, voice low. "Or did you forget that already?"

"Sorry, Ma'am," Gerty says. "No Ma'am."

Hunt sighs. "Okay, look." She straightens, surveying the entire room, even Alyx. "I don't want this to be a suicide mission. This is a simple search and rescue, then assist. I do not want anyone hurt. I want you all coming back alive. And let's just forget my status right now." She tosses a twisted star on the table. It makes a metallic clank on the hard surface. A badge all generals carry. "I'm not your General right now. I'm speaking as a fellow human. I'm speaking as your friend. Be careful out there. Watch your back and each other's. Put aside your differences and find our people."

Everyone just sort of glances at one another and Alyx almost feels a bit of respect for Hunt. It's probably all an act, but it's a good one. She seems sincere. Besides, they're all in her hands now. She's responsible. Unless this is all a bunch of shit and it truly is a suicide mission in the name of science. These days, Alyx has seen it all. Betrayal is like the new cool thing.

Finally, Alyx forces herself away from the wall and says, "Thank you, Ms. Hunt." She ditches General because, well, now Hunt is just a woman. No power or authority, just a strong-willed woman. Or at least in theory. Could be just a show to put on for her troops. It's a well-worn tactic. Strip one's authority to look eyelevel with those under you. Let them see you as one of them and they'll listen better. They'll relate.

Hunt gives Alyx a wan smile then addresses the others, "Great or small, we all look out for each other, okay?"

Alyx watches the others nod in agreement, even Captain Row.

Hunt picks up her twisted star and stows it in her pocket. Now she's their General. Just like that. Nice little psychological trick.

And it *was* a trick after all.

Still, there's an almost loving expression on Hunt's thin face. Like she's looking at her own children. "You deploy in one hour. Gather what you wish to take with you and report to Dock 9. Everything else will be provided, including the weapons you'll need. All supplies such as drink water and survival gear will also be included." She smiles. "Now go make humanity proud, as I am proud of you."

The Marines stand and file out of the room without a word. So robotic in their movements. Even rebellious Gerty. Alyx is the last to get to the door and before she can leave, Hunt grabs her arm and tugs her back.

"Dr. Wick, Alyx, please sit for a moment longer."

"Shouldn't I stay with the team?"

Hunt shuts the door and motions for Alyx to sit at the table.

Alyx sighs and sits in the nearest chair.

To her surprise, Hunt sits right next to her. Not opposite, or standing.

Hunt sighs. "Can I be honest with you, Alyx?"

Alyx blinks. "You mean you haven't so far? Well…shit…"

"Don't be an ass. I'm trying to talk to you person to person."

"Ohh, you're doing that, 'I'm not a General right now', thing." Alyx winks.

Hunt snorts. "I'll always be a General. I'll retire a General. But that's just my job. Unlike most, I can separate my work from life. I can detach from my job. That's what I'm doing now."

"Are you?"

"Yes. Alyx, please, I'm really not your enemy here. I want you to be safe. I want you to come back with everyone. Dr. White and Company 3. I want you all back and I won't leave you out there alone. I'll give you four days. If coms go down during that time I will send a full assault recon team to retrieve you. That's a promise."

"A full, *assault* recon team? Well, holy shit. All for little ol' me?"

She watched Hunt's expression fall from warm to stony. "And for everyone stuck on the planet. I like you Alyx, I really do, but you're being a bitch."

"Then why the fuck didn't you just send that assault recon team yesterday to get Sully and Company 3? Why bother with me or this other team, which, sorry to say, seem like amateurs to me." It all just rolls out of her mouth before she can stop it.

"Because we need that artifact," Hunt says, leaning back a little, her gaze wandering. "This planet is all used up." She looks at Alyx again. "We're dying here. You, me, everyone. We just don't know it yet."

For the first time, Alyx believes she's seeing the true General Hunt. The one she keeps hidden deep. Perhaps even one she thinks is dead, until times like this. Tears well in her gray eyes. Her mouth turns down and she turns away from Alyx a little.

Finally, Hunt sighs, wipes away stray tears trickling down her thin face and says, "I'm not doing this for me, or the Government. I'm doing this for humanity. There are so few of us left, and our numbers are dwindling by the day. Soon we'll be extinct."

Alyx opens her mouth, closes it, then says, "Good riddance."

"No, Alyx. Most of us *are* good. We *do* good. Some of us fall, yes, but we rise again and again. Brighter. Stronger. I want to save us, Alyx, and you're the only one I trust to help me. You and my Marines."

Alyx nods. "Okay. Fine." She stands, gives Hunt a glare. "Four days. I have your word?"

Hunt stands, holds out her hand. "You have my word, *and* documentation of this conversation. Which has been sent directly to your beacon, my office, and the Head of Military Defenses."

Hesitating for only a second or two, Alyx takes Hunt's hand and shakes it.

When they part, Hunt says, "Now, let's save the human race. What do you say, Dr. Wick?"

Alyx shrugs. "I say let's get this shit over with."

Hunt smiles, pats Alyx's shoulder and ushers her out of the briefing room.

Less than half an hour later, Alyx has her suitcase and slips into more comfortable clothes. Her real work clothes, she supposes. Jeans, black T-shirt covered by a leather jacket, strong, black boots and to top it all off...the old baseball cap. With her hair cut short, she doesn't need a ponytail, thank whatever gods there are. Once upon a time she had long hair. Complete frustration. All of it gets in the way constantly, no matter how tight you secure the damn ponytail. She straps on her belt, holsters her gun and joins the others at the docks.

As the Marines, all decked out in their very best body armor and tactical gear, file into the cruiser, all Alyx can think about is Sully.

If he accepted the mission, then it must have been a noble decision.

And she can't think of anything more noble than saving the human race.

SIX

"Close your chambers and prepare for hyper sleep," a robotic voice blares inside the cruiser.

"Best sleep I ever got was in hyper," Gerty says, strapping herself into the white chamber tube next to Alyx.

"Never tried it," Alyx says, hesitating before climbing into the chamber tube. "I like knowing what's going on."

Gerty chuckles, "Hun, trust me, if this bitch explodes out there, you'd rather be asleep than aware of anything."

"Well, no shit. But this cruiser is a jaunter. We'll be at our destination in less than a day. We really need hyper sleep?"

Securing the final strap across her chest, Gerty says, "Look at it this way." The young Marine looks at Alyx, smiles. "You might not sleep at all once we get there. This is like a…" She waves a hand. "I dunno, one of those nice, healthy siestas, or something. Get ya nice and rested before all hell breaks loose." She winks at Alyx, then shuts her chamber.

On the other side of Alyx is Captain Row. She nods at him. He doesn't nod back, just secures his straps, glares, and shuts his chamber against her.

"Well excuse *me* all to hell," Alyx says.

"Dr. Wick," the robotic voice sounds, startling her a bit. "Secure yourself in the chamber, close the hatch. We are about to launch."

She sighs. "Yeah, yeah. Hold your shit, I'm going."

She straps herself in, draws in a breath, and shuts the hatch to her tube.

In here…it's so quiet she can hear her own heartbeat. Which is maddening.

Yeah, fuck this. She goes to open the chamber when her vision blurs. Her hand falls away from the latch as her eyelids droop. Her head is a ball of gauze.

She has a moment to think, *Did I leave the furnace on*? Then she knows nothing more.

In hyper sleep, there are no dreams.

Only darkness.

SEVEN

There's no time to think.

Before her brain can fully wake up, she's being hauled out of the chamber tube. Rip is in her face. He's shouting something, but all she hears is ringing. Her vision blurs in and out. Beside her, also yelling at her, is Row. His scarred face drawn with concern. The world around her shakes.

What the hell is going on? What...

"—she hurt?"

Alyx isn't even sure who said that, but the ringing disappears, thank whatever ugly gods there are out there.

"Just get her outta here. I'll inform Hunt of our situation." That's Row, Alyx is pretty sure, even though she hasn't looked at him to make sure.

"You just make sure you're careful with her, Rip." Yes, this is Gerty. Gerty suddenly cares about what happens to her.

What*ever* is happening to her, that is. Because right now everything is an insane whirlwind of madness.

"I got'er," Rip says.

Then Alyx loses a section of time. A giant, blank, white space where all there is...is silence.

Gradually, the white space of nothing fades. Voices create a mongrelized version of a very strange language that never existed. They echo, these voices. They merge and dance before Alyx like a damn musical void of bodies. Kind of creepy.

Then, a single voice breaks through. "Dr. Wick? Hey! Wake up."

She knows this voice. A woman. Gerty? Yes.

There's a sharp cracking sound and a brilliant surge of pain and—

Alyx's eyes flutter open, and as her vision clears she stares up at Gerty's slightly frustrated, angsty face.

"Well it's about damn time. Christ, lady." Gerty moves away and Captain Row comes into view.

"Can you stand, Dr. Wick?"

"I...don't know." And Christ, her tongue feels like a thick strip of old carpet. "What happened?"

Row and Gerty help her sit up. For a moment, everything tilts and fogs over, then finally clears. She blinks at thick, bluish foliage.

"We kinda crash landed," Gerty says. "Luckily Rip's chamber cracked so he woke up in time to get us all out before shit got real."

Alyx frowns at the younger woman. "So the cruiser is—"

"Broken," Row says. "But Hannah thinks she can repair the damages. Nothing too major. I already spoke with Hunt about our situation."

Massaging her temples, Alyx snorts. "Bet she was helpful."

"She's giving us an extra day to see if Hannah can repair the cruiser in case we need an emergency exit. While she's working on it, we're going start our search for Company 3." Row sighs. "I doubt we'll find them in all this, though. We didn't land in their last known location. We're off...quite a bit."

"How much is a bit?"

"Measuring in miles, over fifty. At least."

"Well, shit," Alyx says.

"We got all the gear out before the fires started too," Gerty spouts. "Thank god."

Alyx's eyes widen. "Fires?"

Rip crouches next to Gerty. "Nothin' too bad. Gerty here is being over dramatic again."

Gerty glares at him. "I hope you fall down a well, or something."

Rip chuckles and pats her shoulder. "Love you too, kid."

Alyx glances around at all the dense, bluish foliage again. "So we're stranded?"

"Not exactly," Row says. "Hannah knows what she's doing. And Hunt knows where we are. She's already deployed a rescue cruiser, just in case we don't let her know all is well in time."

"Well," Alyx says. "That's good then."

Row nods. "Get ready to move out." He hurries away, making sure the other Marines are geared up.

Alyx finds her bag, snugs into her jacket and ballcap, then straps on her belt and holster. At the bottom of her bag is the revolver. She makes sure it's fully loaded, slips it into the holster and pockets a few more rounds. Just in case. There are more dangers here in this unknown planet than she's used to. The Marines would protect her, but...there's always a chance...

And she couldn't afford too many chances. Not here in this strange place.

The Marines, seven in all, stand alert at the edge of the dense foliage, Z91's at the ready. Those rapid-fire guns scare her a little. She's heard stories about their power and accuracy. She's heard entire crowds being mowed down by one in seconds. But, if anything can stop whatever roams the woods beyond, then those guns can. Or at least slow it down.

"Company A, ready?" Row says.

"Oorah," the Marines spout in unison.

Alyx smiles. The Marines were a cool branch of the military. Like family, all of them. And she kind of liked that.

She just hoped she was part of the family now too.

"Move out," Row says in a growly voice and motions for the Marines to enter the woods. They do without hesitation.

Row glances at Alyx and nods. "Go ahead, Dr. Wick, I'll follow behind you."

She doesn't say anything, but does as the Captain says. He knows what he's doing in such situations. Even so, she hates being ordered around by a man. It takes more effort to follow the order than it should. Typically, she's the one in charge. It's her that will lead. Then again, if she wants protection, she needs to do as Captain Row says. Like it or not, the Marines are her guards and their respect is key. She might really need them later on.

Pushing into the dense, blue woods, she spots Gerty waiting for her. The younger woman lifts an eyebrow, as if saying, "You coming, or what?"

Alyx sighs and gestures for Gerty to keep moving, and Gerty does.

Behind her, Captain Row follows. His stealthy movements just little more than unsettling and she doesn't know why.

She turns her focus to Sully. If the calculations are correct, they should arrive at Sully's last known location in about fifty miles. It feels like forever away, especially on foot. Fifty miles of blue woodlands and dead leaves crunching under her boots. All around her odd squealing sounds echo through the canopy. Birds? Maybe...

The smell here is also odd. Nothing fresh, like most of the woodlands she's explored smell. No. There's something slightly sour here. An underlying stench of putrescence she doesn't care for. What was it the one Marine called this planet? Dead World? Yeah, maybe that's closer to the truth than Hunt's "New World".

Eventually, Alyx catches up with Gerty. The young woman, she doesn't look at Alyx. Barely acknowledges her presence. Alyx keeps needing to remind herself that this woman is a Marine. A tough as nails soldier. Gerty isn't ignoring her, but being professional. Maybe trying not to get too close. Less emotional connections if you just ignore someone.

Still, Gerty says, "Don't talk too much, if that's what you want to do. Short bursts of convo."

Alyx nods. "Gotcha. How old are you, kid?"

Gerty rolls her eyes. "Don't call me kid, lady. I'm twenty-five."

"Sorry."

"No worries, hun. Now, shh, for a while, okay?"

Alyx nods, liking Gerty probably more than she should.

Ahead, the rest of Company A fan out about four feet apart. A simple strategic formation, Alyx realizes. If attacked, they have enough space to maneuver and defend. But so far, there's no sign of anything except for the birds, or whatever, squealing in the trees. No sign of life. Which makes Alyx wonder why? Where are all the wildlife Hunt warned them about?

Maybe the General's scans were off.

It happens. Even with the military.

Not that it's a bad thing, really. It's good. This way they don't have to fight off any predators and just work their way to Sully's last location. At this rate, they should be there in no time. Well, more or less.

The heat in the woods is tolerable. Nothing like a jungle. Or tropical. Maybe a steady eighty degrees. Not much humidity. She's sweating a little, but that's to be expected.

The land slopes downward as they trek onward through thick brush. The putrid stench remains as they go, as if death itself is clinging to them.

After an hour or so, Gerty hands Alyx a canteen of water from her pack. "Just a couple sips."

Alyx nods and swigs down more than a couple sips, suddenly aware how thirsty she is. Gerty takes the canteen before Alyx can take another drink. The younger woman shakes her head and returns the water to her pack.

It's a survival thing, Alyx knows, and she should've known better than to be so greedy with the water. There's no telling what the fresh water situation is on the planet. She curses herself for making it appear she's so naive.

She's had to survive weeks on a backwater planet after her cruiser broke down during an excavation of the rare metal platus. That planet, C-T10, it was nothing but a massive death trap. The water there had been so nasty not even purification lasers could make it drinkable. Only thing she relied on was the rain. Which came down in small, wild spurts, but drinkable nonetheless. Fortunately, she managed to fix the cruiser before things got really bad.

The downward slope in the land brings them to a lazy stream.

Alyx stares at it before sighing. "Doesn't look good to drink."

The water flowing over gray rocks is tinted a peculiar orange she's never seen before, but tinted water typically means bad water. At least in her experience.

"Gabe," Row says joining the others. "Gather a couple pots of this. Might be able to purify it."

A man, maybe in his late thirties nods, uncaps two large containers and fills them with the orange water. He screws the caps back on and stuffs the containers into his pack.

"We'll rest here for a few," Row commands. "Rip and Fern, I want you two to keep watch."

Rip and a woman just as tall as him nod and set off in different directions away from the group. Not out of sight, though. Alyx watches Fern, the woman assigned with Rip to keep an eye out, step over a fallen tree and mumble something under her breath.

"Her tongue was cut out when she was ten," Gerty whispers in Alyx's ear.

"*What*?" Alyx turns to Gerty.

The younger woman smiles a bit and stares almost longingly at Fern. "Her father did it. One night she wouldn't stop talking about a toy she wanted for Christmas. He'd been on the liquor pipe most of the day."

"So he cut her fucking tongue out?"

"Oh, for shit sake," Row says, walking by. "Fern's tongue was cut out during the High War by the enemy. We move out in five, ladies."

Alyx blinks, then hits Gerty with a withering look.

Gerty snorts, shrugs. "I would've told you the truth eventually."

Alyx finds herself chuckling, on the brink of laughter. Because, despite everything, she gets the joke. A joke not about Fern at all, but about Alyx. Gerty is just having fun with the new kid. Like a hazing, of sorts.

The joke wasn't very good, but it didn't have to be.

Alyx claps the girl on the shoulder, still chuckling, and walks away. She intends to separate herself from the others. Maybe gather her wits a bit. Since waking up from the fallen cruiser on this dead planet, she doesn't feel right. Her thoughts are paper thin. Her intelligence seems to have fled the atmosphere. Everything that she is feels like it has been skewed and twisted out of true.

Behind her, Row says, "Dr. Wick? You okay?"

Still chuckling, Alyx waves a hand over her shoulder, nods. She can't talk to anyone right now and realizes this is how poor Fern must feel. Wanting to talk and shoot the shit, but unable because something horrible has happened to the tongue. For Alyx, instead of missing the tongue, it's like something between her tongue and mind has been severed. Some primitive link. She doesn't know.

Before long, she's away from the others enough for her to sit down and try to figure out what the hell is wrong with her. Is it being shocked back into the waking world instead of slowly reintroduced? Hyper sleep is a dangerous thing. Even after so many tests and studies on it. The false sleep is said to be perfectly safe these days, but what if there's still glitches? What if waking up too quickly can yank something out of a person that used to define them?

None of it makes much sense.

It's like she's this sentient being simply floating among the Marines and not really adding anything to the search. Like she's just there. A ghost of herself.

Well, it's time to bring everything back together. Not only for her and the Marines, but for Sully. She needs to be whole to keep her wits about her. Needs to be her true self and do what she does best...

Find unfindable things. Find what is said can't be found. She might be a pirate, in a sense, but at least she's a good one. One with *some* morals. Money is money and needing it so badly, she has to do what she can to live. And live as well as possible. The teaching gig is just that. A partial cover up, a bit of extra money to help make life comfortable. Hunt will pay her for this little fiasco, sure, but the military likes to be weird about paying people. Sometimes it happens, most often it doesn't.

Yes. She's good at what she does. And—

"Well, Dr. Wick, fancy meeting you here."

Her eyes widen. "No."

She looks up into Vilas's grinning, old man's mug. His teeth are perfect. White and even. Not natural. Not real.

"Greetings, Dr. Wick. How's working for an honest paycheck treating you?"

Gah. That smug, cultured tone of his. She draws her revolver and points it at the old man's head. "Not as great as blowing a hole in your fucking skull." And as an afterthought, "Ready to give back the Sythilias now?"

Vilas chuckles in his most pompous sounding chuckles. "Ah, come now, Dr. Wick. Nothing personal with that." His eyes turn dark. "You need to learn, what's yours is mine, that's all."

"You're a theif."

"And you aren't? Come now. You *stole* it from that sacred temple. Let it go, Dr. Wick."

Alyx pulls the hammer of her revolver back with a ratcheting click. "I will when you're dead."

The old man snorts, shakes his head, and glances over Alyx. "Tell her to put that thing down, will you? She's over-reacting again."

She shoots a glare over her shoulder, spotting Captain Row standing no more than five feet behind her. How long has he been standing there? She never heard him approach.

Alyx stands, sidestepping away from the men. "The shit is going on here?"

Row sighs. "Alyx, Vilas has agreed to assist us in the search for Company 3."

"Does Hunt know about this?"

Row smiles gently. "She's the one who commissioned him."

"What? *Why*? This slime has no clue what he's doing. He takes credit for other people's discoveries."

"She's just mad I found the ancient Sythilias before she did." Vilas flashes his perfect teeth at her.

"Oh for fuck sake. *I* found the Sythilias!"

"Not at all. I—"

"Enough," Row boomed, silencing them both. "I don't know what a Sythilias is and I don't care. What I do care about is finding Company 3 and bringing them home safely. What I care about is the welfare of my platoon. What I care about is doing my goddamn job. So when you two are done bickering about bullshit, let me know. We're out of here in two minutes."

Row turns and tromps back to his small platoon.

"Well, how about that," Vilas says. "Looks like we're a team on this one."

Alyx grabs Vilas by the collar of his crisp, camouflage jacket and yanks him close to her. She presses the muzzle of the gun to his cheek. "You listen to me. This is about finding my colleague, not about fame and fortune. Stay out of my way or I'll blow your damn, smug head off."

Vilas chuckles and pulls out of Alyx's grip. His eyes are wide, almost wild. "It's always about fame and fortune, Dr. Wick." He straightens his jacket, clears his throat. "But I'm not here for that either. I'm here to offer my assistance."

Alyx laughs, holsters the revolver. "And what kind of assistance might that be?"

Again, Vilas flashes her those perfect, white teeth. "Follow me, dear."

He turns away and she holds back everything she has not to bash his skull in with the butt of her revolver. Still, she follows the old fool. Curious, despite herself. They climb a mild slope up to a small clearing and...

"What...?"

Vilas claps Alyx lightly on the back. "The best money can buy, my dear. The Sythilias paid for most of it too."

She's so rapt, she doesn't even try to shoot him over the comment. Because what stands before, her everything they need (and more) to commence a thorough search. There are gliders, monitor equipment, armies of drones for both land and air, an armored trailer, and a few men whom looked tougher than the Marines, if that was even possible. Mercs, more than likely. Because of course they are.

When Alyx finally catches her breath, she manages, "When did you get here?"

"Arrived yesterday. Just waiting on you and Company A to begin."

She looks at him. "So, you knew I was involved?"

Vilas nods. "Of course. You were in the files Hunt let me review. Decided to let bygones be bygones. You should do the same, Dr. Wick. We have the same goal this time. And I assure you I won't steal Dr. White from you." He winks, but his joke falls flat. At least to Alyx anyway.

She still wants to punch his smug face in, but this time he seems genuine in the shared goal. She just hopes Hunt didn't pay him more than he's going to be worth. Because even with all the gadgets, it takes an explorer's imagination to find things. To see outside of the box, rather than being trapped inside.

"Jumpin' shit weasels," Gerty says behind Alyx. "This shit is bananas."

Alyx shoots a smile over her shoulder at the girl.

Row steps in front of everyone. "I received communication with Hannah back at the cruiser. She has everything mostly repaired and it should be ready for our departure once we return."

"Fuckin' A," Gerty spouts.

"General Hunt has deployed a rescue team, which will hover near the planet's atmosphere if we need it." Row points at Vilas. "This is Vilas Carvious. Yes, that one. And he's here on commission to assist out search. As you see, he has a few things to aid us here."

"What about the lifeforms we were warned about?" Alyx watches Row carefully as he responds.

"The scans are accurate, but according to Lance over there, the animals are migrating away from us. We're not sure why, but that's the reason."

Lance is an older man, maybe in his middle forties. Only one older in the group is Vilas and Row. The thing that sets him apart from old man status is the monitor constantly in front of him. And Row doesn't act very old. The only true old man is Vilas. Old and ugly.

"Each of us gets a glider and will be followed by Vilas in his…whatever that trailer thing is."

"Tracker," Vilas, says, smiling.

Row nods. "Okay, he'll be following in the Tracker. His men will join us as added protection. Now, let's move out. We still have a lot of ground to cover before the last known location of Company 3."

Everyone gravitates toward the gliders, which resemble motorcycles in design, though hover over the ground about two feet. They also come equipped with brush cutters that snip off anything that will get in the way. Alyx has never ridden one before, and she's slightly terrified.

She's inspecting one when Vilas says, "Just like riding a bike, dear. Hop on and it will do the rest. Your throttle is on the right handgrip. Brakes on the left. Just like a bike. Everything else, it will do for you."

"Thanks," Alyx says. She sighs and gets on the glider.

The small monitor set near the handlebars scans her weight, body type, and eyesight. The seat adjusts itself, conforming to her. She watches the others get on their gliders without hesitation. Apparently, she's the only one who hasn't driven one of these things.

Figures.

Over the whirring of the gliders, Row shouts, "We have a good forty miles to go. Let's move out and find our brothers and sisters."

"Oorah," the Marines yell.

Then Row takes off in the lead, Alyx follows close behind him, not wanting to be last. When they arrive at the location, she wants to be one of the first people to see it. She needs to get a grasp of it before everyone clouds her thinking.

EIGHT

After a while, Alyx comes to love the glider. It's weird at first, but eventually she gets the hang of it and is soon gliding along without any worry at all. The woods slip by and all she can think about is why Vilas would help the military. There has to be more in it for him than the money.

Is it the artifact Hunt wants? The thing that can create a new world? She's still not sure how that's possible, but people like to believe in what they want.

Though it must've intrigued Sully, otherwise he wouldn't have accepted the mission.

Surely Vilas won't be stupid enough to take the artifact for himself when it's found. The military will hunt him down and kill him for it. Especially if Hunt wants it so bad. Then again, it's Vilas. He's greedy, but not stupid. No. Not at all stupid. He's the most cunning of snakes and Alyx has to remind herself not to enjoy the glider too much. It's just part of the old man's show.

They're about ten miles to their destination when someone says through the glider's COMM system, "Incoming lifeforms ahead." Alyx assumes it's Lance. Probably is.

"Slow gliders down to five," Row commands.

Alyx fumbles with the brakes until the glider begins to slow. And when she comes up on Row way too fast, she clutches hard on the brakes. The force about bucks her off the glider. Thankfully, it doesn't. She's done making a fool of herself. She quickly accelerates until the number 5 flashes on the monitor.

"Lifeforms are large," Lance says. "I recommend we hide and see what we're dealing with before contact."

"Roger that," Row says. "Company, seek the heavy brush. Turn off the gliders. Only shoot if the lifeforms attack. Otherwise, stay quiet until I give the command to move."

Almost in unison, the Marines say, "Roger that, Sir."

Alyx follows Row's lead into a strand of dense foliage. She shuts the glider off and waits.

A moment later small trees crash over in front of Row. Something groans. A deep sound that vibrates Alyx from the inside out like standing too close to a giant speaker pumping out bass. A gut trembling sensation.

The groan is followed by another. Bluish leaves seesaw around Alyx. The world is a mixture of thumps, and groans and she has yet to see the creatures responsible for it all. In her earbud, Row whispers, "Lance, where are they?"

"Right in front of us, Sir."

And that's when Alyx spots one. A massive creature standing about thirty feet that appear to be a mixture of a lizard and gorilla. The way it walks, it uses its front arms, very much like an ape, though its long body is covered in iridescent scales. Its head has a muddled vulpine shape, long, curved teeth poking out from the upper jaw. Its black eyes swivel in their sockets like the ancient lizards she read about in books. Chameleons. A long tail sweeps back and forth as it lumbers through the woods, knocking down trees. In its wake follows another creature of the same origin, yet slightly smaller. A strange, clear liquid seeps from the corners of its eyes, as if it's crying.

After a few minutes, the creatures disappear into the woods and Row gives the go ahead to keep gliding.

Lance says, "No more lifeforms detected."

"Roger that, Lance," Row says.

The woods zip by and Alyx isn't sure what to think right now. With Vilas joining the search, she's more than a little suspicious. It wouldn't be a problem, except Vilas is an asshole. A cheat. A real thief taking credit for things he didn't find. She has to hand it to him, though. He achieved everything she wanted, even if he did it the wrong way. Maybe she would've ended up the same, if not for the sliver of morals stabbing her every time she thinks about stealing from other explorers.

Morals are also assholes.

She's thinking about ways to expose Vilas for what he really is when something clanks against the side of her glider and sparks fly into her face. She screams, squeezing the brakes and swerving away from Row and the others. The glider banks off a large rock. Something under her explodes. Heat burns her legs.

The next two seconds slow down to a crawl as her gaze lifts to the huge tree directly in front of her. The tree that will end her life right here and now and—

Alyx is yanked off her glider and swung sharply around. Before she can comprehend what's happening, Rip is telling her to breathe. He's telling her to hold on to him as her glider explodes into the huge tree.

"She good, Rip?" That's Row.

"Aye, Captain."

"Stop that."

"My bad, Sir."

If Alyx hadn't almost died, she might've howled with laughter.

"What hit her?" Gerty asks.

"Dunno," Rip says. "Blood all over my glider's shield, though."

"Just a small animal then," Row says.

"I registered no lifeforms," Lance says in monotone.

"Well, there sure as shit was a lifeform," Rip spouts.

"Maybe it moved too fast to register."

Rip chuckles. "We got some little critters out there, guys. Stay alert."

"Almost to destination," Row says. "Stay focused. All of you."

No one responds, but Alyx is sure they all heard. Her sights glance over the woodland whipping by. Little critters, Rip had said. But was it mere chance, or is something trying to stop them?

Not all predators are giants.

Not all are monsters...

Still, as they make their way through the woods, no one else's glider is attacked. So, maybe it had only been chance after all.

She shoves it all out of her mind for now. She's had her fair share of near death experiences and it's best not to dwell on them too much. It will drive one to madness otherwise.

"ETA in ten minutes," Row announces in her earbud.

Well, she has to give Vilas credit, the gliders cut away all the time constraints. In no more than two hours after they crashed, they'll be at Sully's last known location. Finally. Then the real search can begin.

"Upon our arrival," Row says. "I want all of you to be on high alert. There's no tellin' what waits for us there."

"No lifeforms," Lance interjects.

A long sigh. "Thanks, Lance."

"Welcome, Sir."

Row clears his throat. "Anyway. I want professionalism the moment we stop. I want Company 3 found and safe before nightfall."

"Tall order, there, Sir," Gerty says.

Row doesn't acknowledge her and falls silent.

Alyx kind of feels sorry for Captain Row. For being the leader of an elite platoon, he has to deal with smartasses daily. Gerty and Rip being the worst of them. Row has patience. Which is a good trait to have as a leader, but damn...

They burst through a thicket into a sprawling clearing that's almost a meadow. If a meadow is made of all rocks, of course. A few miles away stand what appear to be mountains.

"Halt," Row says. "Stay awake, people."

Rip stops the glider and dismounts without a word. Alyx follows, though not sure what the hell she's supposed to be doing yet. Does she gather with the Marines, or stand back? She chooses a happy medium, standing somewhere between Row and the others. Vilas saunters over from his Tracker a moment later. And Christ, the douchenozzle is already grinning. His shiny, high-end boots crunch over the rocks.

"I want you all to spread out," Row commands. He paces back and forth in front of his small elite platoon. "We are on search and find mission right now. I want you all to keep all your senses about you. The tiniest clue, I want it reported directly to Dr. Wick or myself. Understood?"

"Oorah!"

Row nods. "Now get outta here and let's find our missing brothers and sisters."

The Marines wander off in different directions. Fern nudges Alyx. She nods toward the mountains. At first Alyx doesn't know what the tall woman means, then it dawns on her. Fern is offering to be her escort during the search.

Alyx smiles and nods. "Sounds like a plan."

Fern smiles and starts off in the direction of the mountains. It's not where Alyx wants to begin her search, but it'll work. Shit, for all she knows there will be a major clue out in that direction. No matter how much of a waste it appears to be.

The air here chills her sweaty skin a bit. The eighty degrees is now somewhere in the upper sixties. A guess, but she figures it's a close one judging by the chilly breeze. She zips her jacket up and follows Fern.

The rocks crunch and roll under her boots like living things. She catches the whiff of oranges in the air, even though there's not an orange tree in sight. Alyx keeps her sight panning, trying to take in everything, picking out inconsistencies. So far all she sees are stones of various shapes and sizes. Here and there huge boulders dot the landscape.

"So," Row says sidling up beside her.

Alyx nearly punches the dude. "*Shit*. Really?"

Row smiles. "Sorry. Didn't mean to scare you."

"I about shot you, damn it."

He chuckles. "I bet."

"What's up, Captain Row?"

"Oh, I was wondering what you make of this."

"This? Gotta be more specific than that, Captain."

"Call me James."

"Well, shit, you gotta be more specific than that, *James*."

"Sarcasm noted."

"Good." Alyx grins.

Row sighs. "I mean, this place. It's all flat and rocky. Where would a platoon of Marines go around here?"

"You think Hunt's scans are off?"

"Maybe a little. Yeah. It just doesn't make sense that this is their last known location."

Alyx glances at him. She eyes all the scars on his face. "Why is that?"

He shrugs. "Because what they were looking for is underground."

Alyx skids to a stop, eyes widening.

Row frowns at her. "What?"

"That's it," she says, gaze lowering to the rocks.

"Dr. Wick?"

She faces him. "Underground. We're not going to find anything up here. They were *under* us."

Row blinks, then, slowly, his own eyes widen. "Oh. Oh, shit."

"Why didn't I think of that before?" She glances around. "There has to be a tunnel entrance around here somewhere. Tell them to look for that."

The Captain nods and relays the message to the others. When he's finished, he says, "You don't trust Vilas, do you?"

"Nope. He's an asshole."

"I take it you don't believe people can change?"

"Some can, not him, though." She drifts away from him, not wanting to answer any more questions. For one, she's not entirely sure she can trust Row either. For two, she wants to find Sully. Which means she must find a tunnel entrance. And chatting with Row is distracting her.

And yet, the man matches her pace. "Why? I mean, he's helping us out quite a bit here."

"For his own gain, I'm sure. Now, Captain Row, if you'll excuse..."

She pauses, staring at one of the nearby boulders.

"What? What is it?"

"Shh," she says, walking to the boulder.

For a wonder, the man shuts up as she inspects the boulder.

Something caught her attention, but this close up, she can't find it. She can't...

Alyx turns to her right, eyeing the boulder sideways. A smile spreads over her face. "There you are."

In his throat mic, Row says, "Marines, to me."

Alyx, still smiling, turns to the boulder and places a hand on its rough surface. "Where are you? Where...ah..." Her hand disappears into the boulder. She grasps a lever and pulls.

The ground under her trembles. A crevasse around the boulder opens up. The smaller rocks fall, caving in the ground. She backs away as the crevasse widens. Rocks click and clatter as they tumble into the crevasse.

Gerty claps Alyx on the shoulder. "Good one, girl."

"Lucky is all this is," Vilas says behind her.

This is what the man does. He plucks nerves. Well, she's not going to let him. Not right now, anyway. She needs all of herself as the crevasse widens farther and steps appear.

"You found a goddamn stairway," Rip says. "Holy shit."

"Language," Gerty says, laughing.

"You're one to talk, little one."

"Shush"

They both laugh as the crevasse stops widening.

"Alright, people," Row shouts. "Get the gear. We're going underground."

"Yippee," Vilas mutters.

Alyx turns around to face him. "Have any gadgets for tunnels?"

And for the first time since she's known him, Vilas's smug grin falls away. She savors this for a moment, then makes her way to the top of the stone steps.

"We'll need lamps," she tells Row. He gives the command to equip the lamps and high-density lights. He also hands her a lamp.

Drawing in a deep breath, Alyx begins the cautious descent underground. Her heart thrums and she can't stop smiling. Finally, she's on the way to finding not only her mentor, but good friend, Sully White.

Finally.

NINE

The stairway downward takes longer than she initially thought. These steps, they appear to spiral down into forever. A dark abyss floats below her. And behind her, the rest follows. She's not sure where Vilas is back there, nor does she much care. Absently she hopes he falls off the steps into that forever abyss below. For him to simply disappear into the darkness and be lost forever.

That's what she wishes, but knows damn well that old man is an accidental survivalist. Somehow, he just keeps ticking. Old age can't touch him and accidents seem to veer away. It's ridiculous.

The sound of her boots on the stone steps echo all around them. Topside is but a silver, glowing ring. Underground on this planet meant business. She's going deep. And the darkness swallows her with every downward step.

And just when she thinks the steps will never end, her right boot thumps onto soft, black dirt.

Reaching the bottom, Alyx steps aside as the others join her.

"Whoa," Gerty says brushing by Alyx. "This is kinda awesome." The younger woman sets up a runner. Which is pretty much a motion detector light on wheels. It will light the way until something moves up ahead, giving everyone enough time to ready themselves for whatever might come.

Alyx has never seen one in action before, but the gadget might prove useful.

The tunnel, so far, isn't narrow. Alyx guesses it's somewhere in the region of seven feet wide and about ten feet from floor to ceiling. Down here, it smells like cinnamon. A dry, spicy smell. The air isn't cooler, as she suspected, but warmer than above.

Everyone straps on the shoulder lamps doled out by Lance.

Row gathers his Marines. Fern and Rip flank Alyx like giant sentinels. She's not sure where Vilas is, nor does she care. Maybe he's claustrophobic. One can hope.

"Turn your locators on, people. Including you Alyx. Lance, I want you at point monitoring for movement and lifeforms at any body temperature. We're in the beast's intestines now, boys and girls. And—"

"There are boot prints all over here," a voice Alyx hoped she wouldn't hear. "This was where they really were when the distress call sent. I know it in my bones." Vilas, once more, trying to take credit for a find.

He's somewhere behind the group, but Alyx wants to punch him for being a pompous ass.

Row blinks, gaze drifting to Alyx. He smiles, just a bit, perhaps letting her know he knows who really found this location. Then the Captain says, "The runner will travel forty feet ahead of us. Pay attention to it. If the light goes out, prepare yourselves. Switch from lamps to night vision. You all know the drill."

Softly, the Marines say, "Oorah."

"Alyx, I want you on point with Lance. Your skills are required now." Row nods to all of them and steps aside as Alyx follows Lance to the front of everyone.

A cultured chuckle floats on the dry air. "You're letting *her* up there? We'll be lost in minutes."

"Vilas," Row says in a don't-fuck-with-me tone, "I want you with me following. Just in case Alyx misses something."

"Lovely."

Alyx fights back a laugh. She loves hearing the old man squirm a little. Vilas isn't used to being ordered around and absolutely not used to being second fiddle to anyone. It's about time he's put in his true place and Alyx almost wants to hug Row for doing so.

"I'll walk a couple feet ahead," Lance tells her. "You do your thing, Dr. Wick."

"Thanks," Alyx says.

Lance nods and walks away. She draws in a breath, lets it out slowly and follows, keeping her shoulder lamps on full and sweeping herself back and forth. Her sight scans everything. The dirt floor. The hewn, stone ceiling and walls. Every crack in the walls, no matter how thin, she carefully notes. Her explorer mind switches on, taking the lead of all else. Driving her.

This is what she lives for. The finding of lost things. She doesn't care about the artifact Hunt wants. She cares about Sully. This too, drives her onward. Her senses heighten a bit, as they always do in such cases. Instead of finding a thing, she's looking for a person, which makes her overly sensitive to her surroundings. A person can die. An object won't.

And she fears Sully's time might be running out.

This is if it hasn't already.

Latching onto the possibility Sully is still kicking, she forges on through the gloom of the tunnel, noting so soon how the passage is narrowing. Tapering, for want of a better word. Even if the others haven't noticed yet, she already feels the world closing in around her. Claustrophobia doesn't concern her, though. She's never felt it. No matter what tight situations she's been stuck in, there's never the urge to panic. Never the sickness of being crushed. Even if there's a possibility that she might be buried under mountains of dirt and rock, it never worries her too much.

The dirt floor is soft, like powder. It puffs around her boots with every step. She wonders if maybe the dirt should be tested for toxins, but soon tosses the thought aside. If Row thought it to be hazardous in any way, he would've ordered everyone to put masks on. Or at least she hopes he would. Hard to tell for sure with Row. Hard man to read, she's finding. Nonetheless, she respects him and he might even respect her. An ally like that will be useful if the time comes.

The deeper they go into the tunnel, the warmer it gets. Sweat beads on her forehead and she absently wipes it away. Ahead of her, about four feet, Lance is hunched over his monitor. It makes a sardonic whump-whump sound. Behind her she hears the others breathing. She listens to the creaking of their gear and the swish of clothing.

"So, what are you thinking?"

Heart skipping a beat, Alyx glances to her right to find Gerty there, smiling. Jesus, why do they keep *doing* that? Stealthy bastards.

Calming herself down a bit, Alyx replies, "About what?"

"About this tunnel. You think they're down here, or what?"

"I don't know. But it makes sense."

Gerty nods. "If you say so."

Sneaking another look at the girl, Alyx notes how pale she is, even in the gloom. There's sweat trickling down the sides of her oval face. Her breathing is a bit erratic.

"Hey," Alyx says. "Slow, deep breaths."

The girl shoots her a glare. "Huh?"

"You don't like tight spaces, do you?"

Gerty shrugs. "Had some bad experiences when I was younger, that's all. I'm fine. I mean, I survived the hyper sleep tube."

Alyx focuses on the tunnel ahead. "Think about the sky."

"Huh?"

Alyx smiles. "The sky. Think about how free you are up there. How nothing can stop you. How the air is clear and fresh and open."

"The hell you talking about?" Gerty glances over her shoulder and half whispers, "Row, she's gone nuttybars on us. Can we trade her in for a new one?"

Alyx chuckles. "What I mean is, think about anything that's out in the open. Think about your favorite spot to relax or get away. I had an assistant once. She was terrified of tight spaces like this. But once she taught herself to think about the sky, she did just fine."

"What? She pretend she was a bird or something?"

"Exactly. She imagined herself as a bird. Soaring through the clear blue sky. The point is, separate your fear from what scares you. Detach and soar. It's all in your head."

She waits for Gerty to spout another joke, but instead the girl stares at her for a moment. Alyx refrains from looking at her, but feels the curious gaze.

After the moment passes, Gerty whispers, "Thank you, Alyx." Then she falls back a few steps.

Sometimes all people need are the words spoken to them. Once it all clicks, courage prevails. Usually.

In Gerty's case, the younger woman already has courage, just not the kind she needs in the constricting nature of the tunnels. Hopefully the small talk helps her.

"How far does this thing go?" Vilas being Vilas.

"There's no telling," Alyx says before anyone can respond. "This might be a single shaft leading to a cavern, or a system."

"In non-tunnel dweller terms, please." That's Gerty.

"This tunnel might lead to a big cave or branch off into many other tunnels, like tributaries."

"Rock on."

"If I had known about the tunnels I would've come more equipped," Vilas says.

"I found out less than an hour ago, jackass." Alyx is kind of enjoying this dumber version of Vilas.

"You two done bickering now?" Row sounds more than a little aggravated. "Clear the radio. Both of you."

Alyx adjusts the night vision screen, readying it just in case, and falls silent. With Vilas here, it's like fighting a schoolyard bully. Only instead of meaty fists, he tosses meaty words dripping with condescendence and—

It happens so fast.

A small, white thing latches onto Lance's face. Its long, pale tentacles wrap around him.

"Holy *shit*," someone shouts. Either Rip or Row.

Lance, his screaming muffled, drops to his knees trying desperately to peel the small creature off his face. Using every ounce of muscle she has, Alyx grips onto the pale tentacles and pulls. But every time she stretches a tentacle free, it slips out of her hands and reattaches. Rip and Gerty joins her, both trying and failing to pry the creature off Lance.

"Shit, what the hell?" Rip shouts. "Can't get a good grip on it."

"Look out."

Before Alyx has time to notice, Vilas slips in, stabs the creature with a round, metallic object and shoves her aside. "Everyone move!"

Rip and Gerty leap out of the way a second before the round object explodes. Alyx can't tell from the tunnel floor where she lies what shoots out of the thing, but the creature squeals and falls off Lance's face. It crawls about a foot away before its tentacles curl and twitch. Another second...and the thing stops moving.

"The *fuck*," Gerty spouts, breathing in nothing but gasps. "What the hell was that?"

Vilas helps Alyx to her feet, his face is streaked with concern. Something so alien on his gaunt, wrinkly face.

Lance jitters on the tunnel's floor. The black dirt plumes clouding around him.

Alyx holds him down. "Anyone have medical experience?"

Fern, the tall woman, she brushes Alyx aside and begins CPR on Lance.

"Stay alert, Marines," Row says. "We're not alone down here."

Rip and Gerty step around Lance and focus on the tunnel ahead. The runner has not stopped yet. Somehow the creature that attacked Lance slipped by its sensors. Or...

Alyx's gaze drifts to the ceiling. The stone appears solid. No holes. Same with the walls. The only other way for a creature to sneak by the runner is the floor.

Her eyes widen.

The *dirt* floor.

She grabs Lance, heaving him over her shoulder.

"What the hell are you doing?" Row goes to take Lance from her but she spins away.

"The dirt," she says. "It came from the dirt."

Gerty turns a bit to look at Alyx, eyes wide. "What do you mean?"

Even though Lance isn't a big man, his weight is making her legs tremble. "The thing that attacked him, it came out of the floor. Everyone keep your wits about you."

Row takes Lance from Alyx and this time she lets him. Once the man is positioned comfortably, the Captain says, "I need to get him out of here."

Vilas snaps his fingers and two of his men hurry to his sides. "I'll take care of him. The Tracker is up there, so he'll be safe."

Alyx watches Row's expression droop a little. The man's eyes don't shift away from Vilas for at least a full minute. Then he says, "Okay. Also, I want you to report this to Hunt. It's our check-in time."

Vilas's men take Lance from Row.

"Of course, Captain Row. I'll take good care of your man and check-in with General Hunt as soon as I'm topside."

Row nods. "I want the full recoding of your conversation with Hunt, as well."

Vilas, without pause, smiles and nods back. He snaps his fingers again, turns away and two of his other men replace him. Big, oaf-like dudes with stony expressions Row doesn't appear to know what to do with.

Alyx watches Vilas and his men take Lance away. Watches until they disappear into the darkness. Something tugs on her brain. Something slightly off, but—

"Got movement in the dirt," Rip shouts.

"Guess this planet isn't as dead as I thought," Row says, moving around Alyx, gun aimed at the dirt floor.

She hadn't realized it in the briefing, but he was the one to spout the dead world label. At the time, her mind hadn't made the connection.

"Movement is an understatement," Gert says. "The entire *floor* is alive."

Everyone backs away as the things under the dirt slither closer and closer.

Row thumbs the safety off his Z91 rifle and shouts, "Kill'em all!"

Gerty, Rip, Fern and Vilas's men follow Row's lead, blasting the dirt floor in mad, rapid bursts. Alyx draws her revolver, but doesn't shoot. Not yet. The air fills with the powdery dirt. Already, Rip is coughing from it. The acrid odor of it strikes Alyx's nostrils like a slap to the face.

"Air masks," she says. "The dirt might be toxic!"

But the others don't hear her over the gun-blasts. The tunnel amplifies everything and the sound is deafening. She touches a button on the collar of her tactical vest. A mask rises out of the collar, secures over her mouth and nose, yet still allowing her to turn her head. Fancy, she thinks and nudges Row. He pauses shooting enough to slice an irritated glance her way. She taps the mask.

For a moment, he doesn't appear to understand. The fog of battle does this to soldiers, she knows. Then his expression clears. He nods, presses the blue button on his collar. The mask rises, forms over his mouth and nose. He gets Gerty, Rip, Fern, and Vilas's men to do the same.

However, the distraction is a mistake.

A bunch of the white, tentacled creatures erupt out of the dirt. Alyx shoots as many as she can, their small bodies exploding in gouts of purple slime, before a couple latch onto Rip and Gerty.

"Wick," Row shouts through the mask. "Take Rip, I'll get Gerty."

She doesn't hesitate this time and manages to pull the creature off Rip before it can really wrap itself around the big man. She tosses it aside with a grunt of disgust, and blows a hole into the thing. She takes a brief moment to inspect it.

It has three, gray eyes protruding out of a flat head, much like a crab. Only its mouth is wide and full of hook-like teeth. Its skin is wrinkly and white, coated with yellow slime. Six two-foot tentacles writhe from the flat body. Sticking out each of these are three inch, ashen barbs dripping with foul-smelling fluid.

"Alyx," Gerty screams. "Look ou—"

The impact is like being slammed in the shoulder by a ten-pound sandbag. Alyx staggers, about loses her balance, and claws at the creature trying to fix itself onto her shoulder. It mewls at her.

Fern shoves her into the wall, clutches a massive handful of the slimy, white flesh, and yanks the thing off Alyx's shoulder. It squeals, tentacles lashing. One of the barbs catches Fern's cheek, tearing a thin groove through the skin. The tall woman growls and literally rips the creature in half. She drops the halves, gives Alyx a pat on the shoulder, then turns to the dirt floor again. Fern squeezes off a few rounds, then begins to list to the side. She bumps into Rip who frowns at her. He shoots a few of the creatures and ushers her behind them.

Row, Gerty, and Vilas's men continue firing and pulverizing the little monsters until the floor stops moving.

And as the dust clears, all Alyx can do is blink at everything. Leaning against the opposite wall, Fern stares straight ahead. Her right cheek is swollen, her lips engorged. Yellow liquid seeps from the cut on her fat cheek. In the high-density shoulder lamps, the cheek is bright red and appears to pulse.

"Shit, what the hell was *that*?' Gerty hurries over to Alyx. "Are you okay?" Her voice is muffled through the mask.

"Yeah. But…" Alyx points at Fern.

Gerty follows her finger and freezes. "Oh. Oh, *shit*."

Row kneels beside Fern, tries to get her attention, but the woman doesn't respond. Just keeps staring at nothing. The right side of her face is so swollen the eyeball bulges out of its socket.

Row presses the blue button and the mask slips back into the collar. Into the small throat mic, he says, "Vilas. Vilas, do you copy?"

And surprise, surprise, Vilas doesn't answer.

"Vilas. We need immediate medical assistance down here."

Nothing.

Alyx kneels on the other side of Fern, getting a closer look at the swollen side of her face. She doesn't want to, but retracts the mask and radios Vilas as well.

"Get your head out of your ass, Vilas. This is serious."

"Maybe the tunnel is interfering with the signal?" Rip glances at the men Vilas left with them. "You guys medics?"

Both men shake their heads, eyes barely blinking.

Alyx stands, walks over to them. "Spit it out. What's his plan?"

The men exchange glances. The blond one says, "To aid in this search in any way possible."

"Right," Alyx says. "Now tell me the truth. Why is he really here?"

Row touches her shoulder. "Give it a rest. They won't talk."

The men once more exchange glances. They say nothing more.

Alyx holsters the revolver, but not before thinking about using it to make them talk. The thought is tempting, though. Vilas is an ass, and he might have turned over a new leaf, yet, she still doesn't trust him. Nor does she buy the no signal thing. A signal should've gotten through just fine down here.

Unless something happened to Vilas. Maybe some creature ate him. And although that'd be fantastic, she worries about Lance.

She faces Fern again, trying to think of a way to help. The woman is pretty much catatonic. As the swelling creeps to the other side of her face, the spot where the tentacle cut her oozes yellow liquid. The barbs are poisonous, clearly, though how does one stop the swelling?

They need to figure out something fast before Fern dies.

Alyx kneels next to Fern again. She touches the red, swollen cheek, not sure what to do, when it bursts and hundreds of tiny translucent things spew out like baby spiders.

Gasping, Alyx scrambles away from Fern.

"Holy shit!" Gerty starts toward Fern. Alyx stops her.

"Don't get near those things!" Alyx frowns at Fern. The woman's head lolls. Her right eye finally pops out of its socket and dangles on her swollen cheek. A gurgling noise issues from the woman's gaping mouth.

"What the fuck are we supposed to do?" Gerty turns from Alyx to Row, until facing Rip. The large man's face is solemn as he shakes his head.

Row sighs. "Burn her."

As the tiny spiderlike creatures scurry down Fern's body, Row says, "Rip, use the fireblast."

"Are you serious, Captain?" Rip says. "She's one of us."

"There's no way to stop it, Rip," Row says. "She's barely living as it is right now. Vilas won't answer my call. None of us are medics. I could patch her up, but she's been impregnated. She's an incubator for them. Nothing I can do will stop that. The only way to assure our own safety is to destroy her and those things."

"That's fucked up," Gerty spouts.

Rip, looking like he's about to vomit for as pale as he is, unclamps another gun from his back and points it at Fern. The tiny spider-like creatures swarm over her body.

"Now, Rip," Row says, his voice gentle as he steps away from the woman.

The big man draws in a breath, flips a small switch on the side of the gun, and pulls the trigger.

There's a bright flash, and in a few seconds, Fern, along with all the baby creatures, are reduced to a pile of dark ash.

Rip secures the flashgun, face like chiseled stone, and turns away. Gerty places a hand on his broad shoulder, but he brushes her off and walks down the tunnel alone.

Row tries once more to hail Vilas, but like before, there's no answer.

"So, what are we going to do?" Gerty asks, staring at the mound of ash and wiping tears from her face.

Everyone's gaze shifts from one to another. Row glares back the way they came, as if contemplating going back.

Stepping in front of them all, Alyx says, "We keep going. We'll gather Fern's ashes and keep going. We have to."

"I'm sorry," Gerty says, face darkening. "But when did *you* become our commanding officer because I—"

"She's right," Row says and moves to Alyx's side. "We finish the mission. Company 3 still might be alive. And even if they're not, we still bring them home to their families."

Rip says, "Oorah."

Gerty sighs, nods. "Oorah."

Vilas's men exchange stony glances, but that's all.

Christ, Alyx thinks. *Are they fucking robots or something?"*

"I'll gather her ashes," Row says. "Then we move out. Time to get this done."

No one says anything as Fern's ashes are sucked into a tube and stowed in Row's pack. Fern deserves some good words, but as Row secures his pack, no one speaks. Silence is all anyone can manage.

And in silence, they mourn.

TEN

"Wait," Alyx says, listening.

A low buzzing sound echoes through the tunnel. A frown creases her face as she steps forward a few more feet, then stops again.

"What is it?" Row asks beside her.

"If I knew, I'd tell you, pal." Alyx sighs. "Sorry. Sounds like a bunch of wasps."

"Wasps?" Rip moves back a bit. "All yours guys." He nudges Vilas's men.

Alyx snorts. "I doubt it's wasps, Rip."

"These guys haven't done anything, though."

And for the first time since the creatures attacked, one of the men says, "We are here to help when needed."

She's not sure which one spoke, but guesses it's the dark-haired douche. The blond one has a more nasally tone.

"Uh-huh," Gerty says. "Heard that one before."

"Just make sure you guys do," Row says. "If we need your help, I expect your help. Got me?"

There's a grunt from one of the men, but that's all.

Ahead, the low buzzing sound continues. Alyx ventures away from the rest, even as Row orders her back. They soon catch up to her, however. Gerty grabs her arm and yanks her back.

"The hell you think you're doing, Alyx? If there's something bad up there we couldn't help you right away."

Alyx pulls out of her grip. "This isn't my first rodeo, hun."

Gerty frowns. "Aren't you a teacher?"

Grinning, Alyx says, "Among other things."

The girl shakes her head. "Your file said Professor of Archeology and Exploration."

Instead of enlightening Gerty, Alyx smiles. She keeps walking as the buzzing grows louder. To her surprise, the girl doesn't keep probing. Call it a Marine's knack for self-control. Or maybe Gerty lost interest. Either way, Alyx welcomes the relative silence. Save for the buzzing, of course. She can think better without the distraction of conversation.

Sharp clacks mingle with the buzzing and...

"You're gonna need a better bot," Alyx says, walking to the runner as it crashes itself into the wall again. The lights are shattered and, as Alyx crouches to take a better look at the thing, there are claw marks gouging the metal body. White sparks spurt out of the undercarriage.

"Guess this is why it didn't warn us about those things?" Gerty stands nearby, gun pointing at the wall of darkness down the tunnel.

"No. It was still working fine when the creatures attacked. This happened sometime after."

Visibly tensing, Gerty asks, "By the same monsters?"

"I don't think so. Look." Alyx points at the claw marks. "These are too big. And made by claws, not the barbs or teeth of those other things."

"So, there are…other things down here?"

"Looks like it. Row?"

The man taps Gerty on the shoulder. She shuffles ahead a few feet.

Row crouches opposite of her, eyeing the runner. "What do you think did this?"

Alyx shakes her head. "Something not good." She stands. "Keep an eye out for anything even remotely out of place along the walls and ceiling. A blurry area. Anything like that."

"Blurry area? You think whatever did this can cloak itself?"

"It's a possibility." Alyx straightens her baseball cap and steps over the runner as it continues beating itself against the wall. "Let's go."

Row doesn't remind her of who is really running the show. She's not military. She has no authority over anyone. The only edge she has right now is tunnel knowledge and her explorer mindset. This includes a small ability to know when she's being studied.

And right now, as they continue down the tunnel, she feels just that. Something is watching them very closely. Something yet unseen.

Perhaps the runner was a warning.

Then again, she's never heeded a single warning in her life. Why start now?

Come whatever may.

The Marines and Vilas's men crowd behind her as the tunnel continues to narrow. The walls sweat a rank liquid and when Alyx touches it, her fingertips tingle.

"Don't drink anything down," she says, quickly wiping her fingers on her pants. "No matter how tempting."

"Ten-four," Rip says.

She's not sure how long they've been walking when she comes to a T-intersection. The right tunnel appears narrower. A strange, minty odor wafts out of it. The left tunnel is wide, as far as she can tell. Smells like damp stone.

Row starts down the left tunnel without much pause.

"Wait," Alyx says.

The Captain stops, shooting her an irritated expression. All sour looking, like he just chomped into a lemon.

Alyx points at the right tunnel. "This one."

"Um," Gerty says. "That one looks messed up, Alyx."

"It's the one Sully and Company 3 took."

Row, frowning, storms toward her. "How do you know that?"

She points at the boot prints in the dirt, which has gone from powdery to almost muddy. The prints lead into the narrow tunnel.

Frown dissolving, Row nods. "Good catch, Dr. Wick." He walks away from her and enters the narrow tunnel. Rip and Vilas's men follow.

"I—I dunno if I can," Gerty says. "All that sky shit worked in the other tunnel, but this is nuts." The girl's wide eyes and tense posture says so much more than her words. The female Marine is terrified.

"Same rules apply here," Alyx says. "Think of a spacious place you like to be. Someplace soothing."

Already the lights of the others are fading as they continue on. A burst of panic strikes Alyx.

"Plus, this might be the tunnel that opens up to a cavern. You won't be in the tunnel very long."

Gerty rolls her eyes. "You're a horrible liar."

"Okay, listen," Alyx says. "You're a *Marine*. As tough as they come. As narrow as that tunnel is, it's not near as dangerous as facing down a Tilian horde." Tilians are some of the most feared invaders of the galaxy, Alyx knows. As she knows Gerty has probably fought off a few.

"And you use bad examples.' Gerty sighs. "Okay. Fine. Let's do this."

She forges away from Alyx, enters the narrow tunnel, and doesn't look back.

Alyx smiles for a moment, then stops. She frowns at a pale spot on the ceiling above the tunnel. Just discoloration, but is it really? She stares at it for a while before finally deciding to join the others. If something is watching them, sooner or later it'll make a mistake. All things make mistakes. But so far, it's playing things safe.

This tunnel is so narrow her shoulders scrape along the rough walls. A substance resembling cobwebs stick to her coat and cling to her hat. The minty odor is nearly overwhelming. Her stomach churns and her throat works against vomiting. The stench is so bad it actually brings tears to her eyes. She touches the blue button and the mask secures over her nose and mouth, smothering the noxious odor.

The floor crunches under her boots and when she spares a glance, she realizes she's walking over small bones.

"Figures," she says to herself and soon catches up to Gerty.

The younger woman, she's walking slowly, whispering something too low to understand. Her breathing isn't slow or regular, it's all gasps. She's visibly shaking.

"I'm right here," Alyx says. "You're doing great, just keep moving."

The tunnel, it's barely three feet wide. If that. It's close, even for Alyx. The walls are rough, uneven and pocked with baseball sized holes. The bones scattered on the floor crunch and crackle. She's just thankful for the mask cutting out that nasty mint stench.

"He put me in the trunk," Gerty says.

Alyx blinks. "What?"

"He...he wanted me to be quiet. He said I was too loud. Oh, god, I could barely *breathe*!"

Alyx places a hand on Gerty's shoulder. "Hey, I'm here. Just keeping moving. You're doing great."

"You already said that," Gerty says, though her voice sneaks in between rapid breaths.

Alyx fumbles with a response, not that she needs one because...

"It was hot and oh god, I couldn't get out. Something touched my leg and I didn't have enough light to see what it was. So dark in there. So scary. I tried getting out..."

Squeezing the girl's shoulder, Alyx says, "It's okay, hun. Just take slow, even breaths for me, okay? Slow and steady. We're almost out." She doesn't know if they are or not and doubts they are.

"It's not okay! He put me in the *trunk* of his car. He *left* me there all day. I...I..."

The girl lists to the right and Alyx steadies her. "Whoa. Gerty, you gotta breathe, hun. We're not in the trunk, we're right here. We're in this tunnel and there's plenty of room and you'll never be alone. I'm right here."

Gerty leans against the right wall, shoulders rising and falling with every breath. But at least her breathing isn't rapid anymore. It slows gradually and the girl begins to weep.

Holding her from behind in an awkward embrace, Alyx says, "Shh. It's okay. It's okay now."

"S-sorry. My dad was..."

Alyx squeezes. "I know. Just relax, though. I'm right here. You're not alone."

She's dealt with her fair share of people suffering from claustrophobia, and everyone is different. Luckily, Gerty is tough. She might be scared, but her training and strong will help shove her fear away. Besides, the girl had gone through a traumatic experience. From what Alyx gathers, her dad put her in the trunk of the car because she was being too loud. Doesn't make sense to Alyx's brain, but some parents can be the harbingers of serious traumas and mental issues.

"Thanks, Alyx," Gerty says after a moment and straightens. "Don't tell Rip about this, okay?"

"Not a word. But I thought you two were close?"

"We are, he just doesn't know what my dad was really like. He doesn't know the horrible things that man did to me."

Alyx pats the girl's shoulder. "I promise. Not a word."

After a moment or two more, Gerty starts walking again. This time with moreforce. She doesn't falter and moves quickly. So quick Alyx has a hard time keeping pace at first.

"There you two are," Rip says hurrying to them. He glances from Gerty to Alyx, eyes wide. "Everything okay?"

"We're good," Gerty says. "Just a little…claustrophobia."

Rip cups the girl's face in his large hands. "You never told me you were claustrophobic."

Gerty sighs. "I thought I was over it." She cocks a thumb over her shoulder. "Alyx helped me."

Rip smiles, just a bit and gives Alyx a nod. She nods back.

"Okay," Rip says, leading Gerty onward, "let's catch up to the others." He stops and looks at Gerty. "The ceiling gets lower up ahead, sweetie."

Gerty snorts. "I'll survive."

He kisses her forehead, smiles as he steps back. "I know you will. Let's go."

They follow Rip and before long, the ceiling brushes along the top of Alyx's baseball cap. Rip has to hunch over and walk sideways in order to make it through. If the tunnel gets any tighter, he might have some serious problems. Getting stuck is one of the worst things that can happen in narrow tunnels.

This close, cool air filters out of the baseball sized holes in the walls. A sensation Alyx can do without. There's just something creepy about the holes she can't put her finger on just yet. She's too focused on making sure Gerty's breathing remains even. Too worried about Rip making it through okay.

After a few minutes, though, they meet up with Row and Vilas's men. Which is kind of a relief, because as soon as they're all together, Gerty calms down even more.

The tunnel winds back and forth, like a slithering snake, the ceiling getting lower and lower. More jagged. Rocky spikes hang, making the passage lower still and Alyx can't help but think of the time when she was searching for the lost Bromia Stone. A stone said to contain the real Christian God.

The tunnels were much like this, only not as narrow. One had room to breathe better and not worry about stabbing a rock through their skulls. Nevertheless, those tunnels had been wretched. It took her and her two-man crew a full day to find their way through. And when she found the Bromia Stone, it was just a purple stone. No God within, as far as she could tell. The stone, however, fetched her a good sum of money. So...not all bad. Those tunnels, though...

How the others aren't gagging on the minty air right now, is beyond Alyx. None of them wear their masks. It almost makes Alyx want to retract hers. Almost. But that stink is just too much. The last thing she wants is to vomit in the presence of Marines.

Of course, she doesn't care what they think, but having their respect is a crucial survival skill. They have the big guns, after all.

Not that they have to worry about much. True, they've encountered small hostiles, but other than that, the rest of the world seems dead. Or not as dangerous as Hunt led them to believe. Comparing this planet to others she's visited, it's not so bad.

As she walks by a series of holes, a strange hissing noise wheezes out. She pauses, frowning at one of the holes. Her internal warning synapses snap and crackle.

"Guys," she says, but they don't hear her and continue on without her.

Alyx focuses her lights on the holes. The hissing grows louder.

"Shit," she manages. She glances up the tunnel. "The holes! Watch out for the holes!"

Gerty stops, looks over her shoulder. "What?"

Alyx makes her way to the girl. Rip, practically crouching and appearing miserable as all hell, shoots her a concerned expression. Beyond him, Row and the other two stop.

"The holes," Alyx says. "Keep an eye on them."

"Okay," Rip says. "Why?"

Alyx shakes her head. "I...I'm not sure. But something feels wrong. Just stay alert, okay?"

The big man sighs, and tells the others. Row shoots a look at Alyx down the tunnel. One that almost says, "Are you serious?"

She nods, hoping it conveys. It does, because he nods in return. Everyone directs their focus to the holes. The ragged burrows. Yes, that's it. Burrows. Not just your average holes. Something—

It happens fast. A pale snout full of translucent teeth darts out of one of the holes and chomps into Rip's left arm. He roars, pulls away until his back is pressed against the right wall. Alyx draws her revolver, pushes Gerty aside and shoots the thing from the hole. A gout of gray blood splatters Rip. He tears the jagged maw off his arm, panting. After a few seconds, he gives Alyx a thumbs up.

The big man brings out some gauze from the med pouch in his pack and quickly wraps his forearm. Blood drips everywhere, but as far as Alyx can tell, the wound isn't too bad.

"Take some antibiotics too," she says.

Rip frowns, then injects the antibiotic from the med pouch. He replaces the syringe, sighs, and says, "Thanks, Dr. Wick."

"Just watch the holes."

"You think there's more?"

Alyx shrugs. "I don't know. But better to be aware than not, right?"

Rip grunts. "Right."

The hissing from the holes wavers. Alyx eyes those closest to her, but only darkness stares back at her. If anything is inside, it's watching from deeper within. It's waiting for the right moment.

"Shit," Gerty says. "I'm getting sick of being attacked by little creepy things."

"Better than big creepy things," Rip says as he shuffles along.

"Not really, but hey, whatever helps you sleep at night, man."

Rip chuckles as he shimmies through a tighter spot of the tunnel. He makes it through without too much effort.

"You have that flash gun all ready, Rip?" Alyx asks.

"Always. Why?"

"Because, if shit gets real in here, you might need to use it. If I'm right, all these holes are connected, or like a honeycomb. You shoot fire into one and it'll spread."

The big man nods. "Well, let me know when you want to burn the bastards and I'm game."

"You two sound incredibly corny right now," Gerty interjects.

Rip chuckles. "Someone has to do it, since you're stuck in permanent teenage angst forever."

"Go sit on a stalagmite, old man."

Row motions for them to hurry up.

"Guys," Alyx says. "I hate to break up family time, but we're being hailed."

Rip and Gerty laugh and they make their way to Row and the two men. Alyx wants to tell the two to be quiet, but also understands stress relief when she sees it. And both Gerty and Rip appear a little more at ease as Row points at something ahead.

"The tunnel opens up a bit," Row whispers. "Might be the end."

Alyx wants to tell him tunnels like this will sometimes widen from time to time, but decides to keep silent. Another truth about tunnels…they're unpredictable more often than not.

Hissing from the holes in the walls are the only sounds as they venture toward the opening.

Her gaze drifts from side to side as they near the opening of the tunnel.

"Shit," Row says.

Alyx's sight shoots to him and all the air leaks out of her lungs. The man is stuck right where the opening should have been. And now she sees where the confusion came in. The walls are wavy in this section, creating an optical illusion.

One that fooled even her.

Vilas's two men try pulling the Captain out.

"Push," Alyx says. "He's about halfway. It'll be easier if you push."

Without a word, the men turn and shove at Row. His teeth grit in obvious pain.

Then he begins to scream.

Blood spurts from his mouth. His entire body quakes.

Vilas's men back away, bodies stiff, hands up as if they're afraid to touch Row now. As if the man has become a spontaneous disease.

Rip pushes the men out of the way. "Cap?"

Row screams, body jittering, blood bubbling out of his mouth. His eyes are wide, near to bulging.

Rip grabs onto Row's gear and yanks backward.

"Push," Alyx says, but the big man doesn't listen.

Instead he pulls. He places a giant boot on the wall and roars as he pulls and pulls and—

A loud squeal erupts through the tunnel. Alyx blinks at the holes, then looks at Row. His body has gone limp, eyes wide and unblinking as Rip tugs and pulls to free the man.

"Traps," Alyx says. "Why does it always have to be traps."

"Huh?" Gerty slices a glare at her.

Alyx shakes her head. "Nothing." She shimmies by Gerty. "Rip, he's dead."

"No," Rip shouts. "He's just hurt. Help me get him out!"

As the big man tears free of the stone walls, she catches a glimpse of something pale buried into Row's stomach.

"Stop," she yells. "It's a trap!"

Rip frowns, sweat trickling down his bronzed face. "A what?"

Before Alyx can stop him, Rip gives Row's body a final yank. Rip stumbles over his own feet, falling into Gerty. Both of them go down. Row drapes over them.

"Oh god," Gerty shrieks as blood seeps out of Row's gaping mouth onto her shoulder. "Get off, get *off*!"

All Alyx can do is stare as three, white, eel-like tails writhe out of Row's back. Blood oozes. The muffled snaps of bones shudder the air. Another of the tails, this one protruding from Row's stomach, whips wildly. And it's not until a small, bony back leg rips free, when Alyx realizes it's trying to work its way out of Row.

Rip roars, heaving Row off him. The Captain plops onto the floor face first at Alyx's feet, splashing blood onto her boots. She sucks in a sharp breath, as if slapped, and points the revolver at one of the things wriggling out of Row's back.

"Wait," Rip says, his tone growly. He unclamps the flash gun from his back and motions for Alyx to move out of the way.

Gerty joins her and they step quickly away from Row.

"Oorah, Captain Row," Rip says and pulls the trigger.

A bright flash blinds Alyx for a moment, there's a brief crackling sound, some intense heat, then it's all over.

Row, like Fern, is now nothing but a mound of ashes. Rip clamps the flash gun in place and brings out a containment tube. Very slowly, he kneels and sucks up Row's ashes. A single tear trickles down the man's face.

Beside her, Gerty sniffles and wipes most of the tears away before Alyx looks at her.

"He was the best," Gerty manages through sniffles. "A real leader."

Alyx nods. She has to agree. Row proved, in just the short time she knew him, how cool and collected and strong he could be. Also...how caring and kind. The man showed compassion, which is a rare thing for a commanding officer, at least in her experience anyway. Most of them are arrogant assholes.

She lowers her head in mourning.

Rip places the tube with Row's ashes in his pack and clears his throat. "He was the greatest captain I've ever served under. A man that cared and—the hell did they go?"

Alyx lifts her head a bit. "Who?" But then she knows.

She spins around, finding the tunnel empty behind her.

"Those pieces of shit," Gerty says.

Vilas's men snuck away during all the commotion. Either because they were scared, or Vilas called them back. Both conclusions are possible.

70

Alyx faces Rip. "Fuck'em."

He frowns at her, eyes hard as steel.

Then Gerty giggles. "Damn right, lady."

Rip's expression softens. He sighs, shakes his head and releases a small chuckle.

"They were pussies anyway," Gerty spouts.

"I don't think they were here to help us. They're scouts. Spies. They got info from us and how far we made it. Now they're returning to their boss."

"Vilas?" Rip lifts a dark eyebrow. "That old man is playing us?"

"It's what he does," Alyx says. "I tried to tell everyone that."

Gerty and Rip are quiet for a moment, then Gerty says, "We should go kick his ass."

But Alyx shakes her head. "We need to finish this."

Again, the two Marines are silent.

Alyx opens her mouth to maybe speak some encouraging words, when hisses blow out of the holes around her. Scratching noises dance with the hisses.

She gulps down a heavy lump in her throat. "We need to get out of here. Now." She points at the spot where Row got stuck. "Got anything to blow that a little wider?"

"Shatter grenades," Rip says.

"But won't that cause a cave-in, or something?"

Shaking her head, Alyx says, "This is a natural tunnel. It's strong stone all around. Might cave a bit, but not much."

"Even a bit scares the shit outta me, Alyx."

She shoots Gerty a smile. "Trust me."

Without anything further, Rip unclips a blue grenade from his belt and pulls the pin. "You got five seconds. Run like hell. *Now*." He tosses the grenade between the narrow walls as Alyx and Gerty sprint down the tunnel away from it. Rip follows, catching up to them and—

Boom.

The explosion is beyond deafening. It's world quaking. The force of it throws Rip into Alyx and Alyx into Gerty. All three collapse as sharp rocks pummel them. The world is a chaotic stew of pain and confusion.

Then it's all over.

Rip grunts, shaking broken rock off him and removing himself as their shield.

"Well," Gerty says as she stands and dusts herself off. "That sucked."

As the dust settles, Alyx sighs relief. The grenade definitely opened it up, and with only minimal cave-in, a small pile of stones a few feet from her.

Then she sees them.

The creatures from the walls. The ones that killed Row. Or rather, their brethren. Whatever. They lie in tatters all over the broken floor. Gray blood pools on the floor and drips from cracked walls. The smell worse than the minty stench and Alyx almost secures her mask again when Rip says, "With Row gone, I'm next in command."

Alyx says, "Of course. You okay with that?"

"Hell no, I'm not okay with it. Row was the man." Rip shakes his head. "I'm no leader."

"You're more of a leader than you think you are. The way you treat Gerty and I. The respect, that's one of the signs of a good leader. You got this, and we'll follow." Alyx smiles at the man and he smiles back.

"Thanks," he says.

"Fuckin' A, right," Gerty spouts. "Now can we get the hell out of this shitty ass tunnel with its white weasels? Because, damn."

Chuckling, Rip leads the way through the slightly wider passage. Beyond this, the tunnel actually does widen, opening up to nearly the size of the main tunnel. There are no holes in the walls and the air cools down a few degrees. Nothing drastic. But cool enough to be able to breathe easier.

As they move up the tunnel, Alyx listens to the clinking of the tubes in Rip's pack.

Ashes of the dead, she thinks for no reason at all.

Ashes of the dead.

ELEVEN

"Dr. Wick." Static. "Come in, Dr. Wick." Static.

Alyx stops and glances at Rip and Gerty.

"Sounds like the bastard above," Gerty says. "And not the celestial one."

"Yeah," Alyx says. "He's going to feed us a bunch of bullshit now. Ready?"

Both Gerty and Rip nod.

She sighs, and touches the throat mic. "This is Dr. Wick."

A bunch of static follows, then...

"Hello, Dr. Wick. Vilas speaking."

Alyx rolls her eyes. "I figured that out."

More static, then, "I have an update on the soldier in my care."

"Lance," she says.

Static. "I have done both internal and external scans. So far, there's only a high fever. All tests, this far, are inconclusive."

"I see. Why didn't you contact Captain Row of this?"

A long section of static. Then, "I tried. He isn't answering. Perhaps his coms are broken."

If the man was here right now she'd bash his head in with Rip's rifle. "He's dead, like you didn't know."

"Oh no. I did not know that. My condolences."

"Right. How are Tweedledee and Tweedledum doing?"

"Beg pardon?"

Gerty snorts. "Tell him we know about his bullshit. See what he says."

Alyx turns her mic off. "It won't matter. He doesn't care one way or the other. As long as he gets what he wants."

Rip frowns. "Then what does he want?"

Alyx turns her mic back on. "Why didn't you answer Row when he asked for assistance?"

But all that follows is more static. She knows he heard her. She knows he's still listening. As he is, Vilas will ignore everything unless it involves him.

"Is it because you don't care?"

More static.

Alyx shoots Gerty and Rip a cockeyed smirk. "This is what he does."

"I still don't see what he wants out of all this," Rip says.

"Isn't it obvious? He wants the artifact Sully was sent to find, and now I'm here to help find it too. He wants the thing that will give him the most power. An artifact that will create planets...? Yeah, he wants that."

"Then we won't give it to him if we find it," Gerty says. "Easy."

"Oh," Alyx says. "I'm sure he has a few tricks up his pompous sleeve."

As she finishes the sentence, the tunnel widens, yawning like a massive mouth. The tunnel floor becomes a solid slab of stone. A platform. Here, the air is fresher, though the same cool temp of the tunnel. Well, more or less.

"A cavern," Alyx whispers. "Nobody talk too loud until I get enough light to see what's around us."

Neither Gerty nor Rip respond. Alyx checks her pack for something that will light up the area.

"Look," Gerty whispers.

Alyx looks at her, then realizes the girl is pointing at something. Alyx stands and notices a pin-prick of light. It's not in front of them, but below. She's not even sure how this is possible. Another optical illusion?

She returns to her pack and finds a single flash flare. A standard twelve hour one. Higher density than a typical flare, it'll work. She tells the other two to be alert and she's about to toss a flare.

Neither say anything.

Alyx pulls the top off the flare. Instantly a bright burst of light blinds her. Looking away, she throws the flare. Eyesight adjusting, she watches the flare tumble down and down into a massive cavern below. They stand on a stone platform and the cavern practically swallows them.

"Holy hell," Gerty mutters. All awestruck.

The flare bounces off a tall spire of a building and...

"It's a city," Alyx says, mostly to herself, eyes wide.

"A city? Underground?" Rip steps beside her. "Why would anyone build a city underground?"

Alyx shakes her head. She's encountered plenty of ancient cities underground, but those were buried over time, not actually built into the stone of a cavern like this one. No, this city was made to be underground.

"I don't know," Alyx says, responding to Rip's questions. "But whoever built is long gone now."

"Then where is that light coming from?" Gerty points at the pin-prick of light the flare doesn't quite touch.

"That's what we're going to find out," Alyx says, looking for a way down. "It's Sully. Gotta be."

"But what if it's not?" Gerty frowns at the large city. "What if it's another trap?"

Alyx doesn't respond, investigating the platform they stand on. There are no stairs. No ladders. Just a stone jutting from the mouth of the tunnel over the city. She pops another flare and throws it as far as she can, trying to get more of an idea how large the city is.

She blinks as the flare lights up the cavern.

Dominating the city is a large temple, or arena. Something resembling the now destroyed Roman Coliseum, only this...it's different. From what she can see, it's a solid round wall around what might be a pyramid of some sort. Maybe. The walls are so high she's not sure what resides in the thing's middle. Might be a pyramid, or some kind of obscure shrine for all she knows.

But...first thing's first. She needs to figure out a way down into this huge, dead city.

Alyx carefully inspects the platform once more.

"So..." Gerty says. "What—"

"Shh," Alyx says and points at the girl. "Just...give me a second."

Gerty frowns, but says nothing more as Alyx crawls along the platform, brushing ages worth of dirt and dust away. There are seams running diagonally across the gray stone. It's not a solid rock, but something someone built. A watchman's platform, perhaps? She doesn't know, but that feels about right. Her gaze follows the diagonal seams to the mouth of the tunnel. She stands, storms by Gerty and Rip to the tunnel.

"What are you—?"

"Shh," Alyx says, silencing Rip.

The seams run directly up the walls just inside the tunnel, stopping at the ceiling. Whoever built the platform incorporated it into the tunnel. Alyx runs her fingertips over each seam, brushing away more dust as she does and...

"There," she says, smiling.

Intersecting two seams about eyelevel, is an octagonal shape. Chiseled into it is a tiny image of the round arena-like building dominating the old city. She blows dust away from it.

"What's that do?" Gerty asks, eyeing the shape dividing the seams.

"This," Alyx says and pushes the octagon in.

There's a sharp click, a low grinding sound. The floor trembles as the seams begin to split open.

"Everyone in the tunnel," Alyx says.

Gerty and Rip join her as the platform seams open and the stones start to shift around. Small chunks of rock and dust fall from the ceiling. The sounds of grating stones fill Alyx's world.

"What's happening?" Rip shouts.

But Alyx doesn't answer him. She watches the shifting platform, hoping she hasn't just killed them all. At any moment, the tunnel might collapse, or the floor give way under them.

Then the trembling stops as the platform stones click into place, forming a series of steps leading down.

For a moment, no one says anything.

As the dust settles, Gerty whispers, "Well holy shit."

"Come on," Alyx says. "I'm not sure if this is on a timer or not."

"A *timer*? Isn't this thing a bazillion years old?"

"No clue, but it's best to be prepared."

Gerty sighs, following close behind Alyx. "Yes, Scout Leader Wick."

Alyx snorts. "Nice."

All three descend the wide steps, which join up with another set made of cobbled stone and perhaps the true way down into the city. The platform is simply a way to join the two and just as she thought, the wider steps grind together, and shift. As they stop to watch, the platform reconfigures itself. It juts above them like a solid shroud against the rain.

"Oh hey," Gerty says. "Now we're stuck down here. Isn't that awesome guys?"

"Your sarcasm is noted," Alyx says, chuckling. "But we'll be fine. If there's a way down, there's a way up."

"If you say so, lady."

"I do."

"What if there isn't a way up?" Rip asks.

"Well, then we're really stuck here. Unless we climb out."

"Sounds like fun," Rip says in a grumbly tone.

"Maybe."

The steps of cobbled stone trail into darkness as her first flare sputters out. Their shoulder lamps are still on and provide enough light to see just fine. As their boots clomp onto each step, she wonders if this is the route Sully took. And maybe, just maybe, that small speck of light in the city is him. Maybe he has a fire going or still exploring and Company 3 are looking for ways out.

She doesn't know, but her heart thrums faster with every step closer to the city floor. It's been years since she's talked to her old friend and mentor. Years where she lost her way a little. A time she thought about money more than the actual discovery of a lost item. Money became her devil in many ways.

Then again, everyone has their devil and sometimes it's not all bad.

She still wants to retire from the life. She still wants to live well.

But right now, all she cares about is finding Sully and bringing him home safely. If he's in this underground city, she'll find him. She just hopes he's okay.

TWELVE

The first thing she notices the moment her boots touch the city's floor is how the heavy dust and dirt is disturbed. As though a group of people walked through it.

"They're here," she says.

"You sure?" Gerty glances around. "Those could've been made by anything and holy hell this place is creepy."

"Here," she points at a few tracks. "Distinct boot prints. Marine issue, am I right?"

Rip kneels, checking out the prints, then nods. "Marine issue tread. Yes."

Alyx eyes the prints for a moment, gaze following them into the city. "Let's go."

Large, stone buildings loom over them. Somewhere in this huge cavern, there's a hollow whistling sound. Like a breeze across an empty glass jug. A hooting noise, almost. The sound gives Alyx a small case of the shivers, but nothing to deter her.

Each building is built tall and wide. The round windows stare at her like empty, black eye sockets. Yes, there's a watchful sense here. Much like she felt in the tunnels above. A waiting and watching sensation prickles at the back of her neck like hundreds of tiny needles. Either it's the vacant buildings surrounding her, or something more, she doesn't know. So far, there's no other evidence of something stalking around down here. No other prints, save for Company 3's. And she knows it's them. Finally, after all this time.

"So where do you think that light was coming from?" Rip asks.

"Deeper in," Alyx says.

"At least we have a path to follow," Gerty spouts.

Alyx laughs a little. "Definitely a bonus."

Gerty makes a weird, shuddery breath. "Anyone get the feeling of being watched?"

"It's the windows," Alyx says, not really knowing, but anything to ease the girl's nerves a bit. Even Marines get uneasy. They're humans too, after all.

"Right," Gerty says.

They walk through the boot deep dust on what Alyx assumes is the main street of the city. The one that's like the lifeline for all commuters. Or once was. It's wide and the buildings on either side might've been shops or homes at one time. Her explorer's heart tugs her toward one of the buildings. Just to look around and perhaps solve part of the mystery surrounding the underground city. Why is it abandoned? Where did everyone go? There are no signs of a fight, or bones in the street. Just...emptiness.

The deeper they venture into the city, the more Alyx wonders what Sully thought of all this. Was he intrigued, as she is, by all the silence and emptiness. Did he want to also figure out why? Or was he so steadfast on finding the artifact that nothing else mattered?

These things, she plans on asking him when she finds him.

And she will find him. Even if he's no longer alive, she'll find him. She'll bring him home.

The buildings on both sides grow taller and wider as they continue on. Ahead, like a dark idol, stands the Coliseum-like structure. The round walled area hiding its own secrets.

"So what do you think?" Gerty asks. "Are they still alive?"

"That's what I'm hoping," Alyx says.

"They fucking better be," Gerty says. "After all this, they better be alive."

"Even if they aren't," Rip says. "We'll bring them home."

His statements mirror Alyx's thoughts almost exactly. At least he's on the same page as her. There's that.

"I wonder what that thing is?" Rip points at the large, round structure.

"A place to avoid," Gerty says. "Can we just hurry up and find Company 3 and get the hell out of here?"

"We're supposed to stay," Rip says. "That's the other part of our mission, remember? Find Company 3 and assist in the exploration."

"Well, that's kind of dumb now, don't you think? After everything, plus we have no way to communicate with Hunt. You burned, Captain Row *and* his communicator."

To this, Rip sighs, though he doesn't argue.

It had been an intense time. Acting before thinking, really. Alyx gets it, but now she realizes how alone they really are right now. Their only link to Hunt is through Vilas. And Vilas is working on whatever new scheme he has going on at the moment. She doubts he even really contacted Hunt.

Still, the General sent a rescue team that's currently orbiting the planet. A just in case measure. Maybe if they don't respond for so long, the team will advance and come looking for them. That's if Vilas doesn't get to them first. She wouldn't put it past the bastard to either lie about everything, or kill the team and fake the reason why they all died. He'd come out the hero either way.

The smell inside the city isn't the nasty mint stench, nor the dry cinnamon odor. It's more like stepping into an old cave. A faint, minerally taste on the tongue and a musty earthy aroma. Nothing horrible. Age has treated this place well. Preserved against weather and time, the city will remain long after all the humans are gone.

This place is immortal and what secrets float here, they float alone in the darkness. Forever lost.

No matter how much Alyx might discover, there will always be secrets left unfound. There will always be these dark, stone buildings built by a civilization no one knew existed. Were they a happy society? Warmongers? As diverse as humanity? No matter how deep she digs, she knows she'll never truly understand the people whom once lived here.

No matter how much she digs, some secrets will forever remain buried.

They come to a six-way intersection. The main street spirals out in smaller streets. Like the tunnels, these resemble tributaries. Every one of them feeding its master.

"Which one do we take?" Rip asks.

Alyx looks around for the boot prints, but, somehow, they've disappeared. They just…stop at the intersection.

"I don't know." But there has to be a direction. Which street would Sully take?

She takes in the beginning of all six streets. They're all the same up until the buildings. All the same, save for one. The street on the far right boasts buildings of a simpler nature. To the point of being rundown, even. She stares at this street for a long time, thinking.

All the other streets, the buildings are tall and strong, indicating their owners were well off. But why does this stick out to her so much? It shouldn't, because Sully could've taken any street. And yet…

Alyx faces the far-right street. The one with the smaller, less attractive buildings. It leads away from the Coliseum, but really, does this matter?

She closes her eyes, dredging up a memory of Sully.

They were on one of their last explorations together on a planet named Resyl. The object they came for was elusive. More so than either of them had encountered. A certain crystal said to restore youth. A thing of legend, really. After months of finding nothing, they came to a fork. One way was clear and wide and a clear stream flowed nearby. The other way was narrow, twisted and every tree and plant appeared dead. It was the classic case, though Alyx didn't see it until Sully said, "Sometimes the darkest road is the right road." They took the narrow, twisted road and in two days found the crystal. It gave instant good health to anyone who touched it, but of course did not restore youth. That wasn't the point, though. The point was they travelled the lesser road and found what they sought.

"We'll go this way," Alyx says, stepping onto the street with the lesser buildings.

"Um," Gerty says. "You sure?"

"No," Alyx says. "But I have feeling."

"A...feeling." Gerty chuckles humorlessly. "Oh, that's encouraging."

"She's been right so far," Rip says.

Gerty sighs heavily. "Fine."

The street is likewise blanketed with dust as the main one, but it's uneven and as she ventures down it, there's feeling of loss here. This street, the ones who lived here, it was a poor place. A place of somber reflection and dismal beliefs. A hard street to live on. The crumbling buildings show her this much. But it's more than that. Sometimes the energy of the dead leaves a residue. And what she's feeling is how they felt during their time here. Sadness, weariness, anger. It all mixes together in a simmering stew within her.

She no longer feels watched, but that's the least of her worries. The sorrow here is worse. And as much as she tries, she can't shake it. As is her nature, she wants to find out why she feels this way. She wants to explore. Maybe after she finds Sully she'll return to these ruins and find what she seeks. Maybe not. There's no telling what the future holds right now.

She's so lost in thought she barely hears the man's voice say, "No."

Nevertheless, she does hear it and stops walking.

"Who's there?" Rip readies his gun, scanning the surrounding buildings.

Okay, so she's not going crazy, at least.

Gerty steps close to Alyx, sweeping her rifle back and forth. Alyx is amazed at the change in the girl. She always appears to be this smartass worrier, but she's really a Marine. She's the warrior. Tough and deadly. The change kind of takes Alyx by surprise. As Gerty's face turn stony and her eyes slowly scan every building around them, she reminds Alyx a little of herself while she's exploring. That ultimate focus.

"I'm coming out. Please do not shoot."

Alyx's eyes widen.

And out from one of the nearby buildings emerges Sully, arms up over his head. As her shoulder lights spotlight him, she nearly gasps at the sight of him. From his white, wispy hair and scraggly long beard, to his tattered, grimy clothing. He looks like some crazy homeless man from out of the shadows. His eyes, however, are not wild. They are the same, calm, steady cool blue as she remembers.

Her heart skips a beat, breath pausing.

"State your name and rank," Rip shouts.

Sully blinks, squints through the lights. "Dr. Sullivan White. Archeologist and explorer."

"No way," Gerty mumbles next to Alyx.

Finally catching her breath, Alyx manages, "S-Sully?"

With his beard, she's not sure if he is smiling or not, but his eyes appear to be. "Alyx."

Heart quickening, she turns to Gerty and Rip. "Put your guns down, guys. It's Sully."

They do, both sharing a similar expression of awe. Slowly, though, Rip's changes to something like suspicion.

Sully walks across the street to Alyx. In his left hand, he holds a cylinder object. "You shouldn't have come here, Alyx."

It's not exactly the reunion she envisioned. She kind of expected Sully to be happy to see her.

"Once I found out you were lost during the exploration, I had to come find you." It sounds stupid to her own ears, but it's out and there's nothing she can do about it.

Sully chuckles, and god, when did he get so old? "I'm not exactly lost, Alyx. Our communicator broke. That's all."

"Then why was the Company 3 commander freaking out? Why did he request an immediate evac?" Rip, he eyes Sully closely as the older man faces him.

"We were not prepared for what we found on this planet. By all accounts, the lifeforms were considered either dormant, or long extinct." Sully sighs. "They are not. Some things still roam the land above, as you might have seen upon your arrival."

"All we saw up there were these huge lizard-like things," Gerty says.

"Those are harmless herbivores. It's the small creatures that you need to look out for, dear."

"Guys," Alyx says. "Remember when something struck my glider?"

"Yeah, but we never saw anything after that until we got into the tunnels," Gerty says.

"Then you were lucky," Sully says. "We were attacked on the second day by hundreds of mammal-like creatures. They moved so fast no one could shoot them and we were forced into a cave. That's when one of the Marines accidently nudged a stone, a lever and the ground opened up under us. Luckily, we didn't fall far."

"Yeah, we met some nasty things in the tunnels over there," Gerty said. "Lost two of our platoon, including our commanding officer."

Sully lowers his head a bit. "I am so sorry for your loss, soldier."

Instead of accepting his apology, Gerty steps forward and grabs handfuls of his dirty jacket. She yanks him close to her. "Because of you, we're all fucked."

Rip pats the girl's shoulder. Gerty's lips press together, forming a thin white line. Her eyes narrow on Sully for a moment, then she shoves him away and steps back. Alyx steadies Sully so he doesn't fall from the force of Gerty's push.

Once he's steady, Sully sighs. "Would you like to talk to Captain Rogers of Company 3?"

Rip's stony expression melts a bit. "They're still alive?"

"Of course. We've been exploring this city for a couple days now. I ventured off by myself, curious about where all the inhabitants went."

Alyx smiles. It's exactly what she wants to find out too.

"I thought you were supposed to be looking for some planet creating artifact," Gerty says, voice low.

"I am, though in order to get an understanding of where we are right now, I need to discover who the inhabitants are and what the Coliseum structure over there is for."

Alyx turns to the giant, looming structure. "Any ideas what it is, Sully?"

"No. There's no way inside, from what I can tell."

"Can you take us to Company 3 now?" Rip's tone is neutral, though his eyes are firm.

"Absolutely," Sully says and begins walking down the street. "They're eating dinner right now, I believe."

Alyx watches him walk away. She watches Rip and Gerty follow and soon follows too. But something feels off to her. Not exactly anything about Sully, but just…something feels slightly askew.

She's pondering this feeling as they make their way down the street and dust puffs around her shins.

THIRTEEN

Company 3 is smaller than she thought.

Four Marines in total. They huddle around a large fire eating packaged meals, their faces solemn. None of them look up as Sully leads Rip, Gerty and Alyx into the small camp.

The fire, Alyx realizes, is the source of the pin-prick of light they all saw on the platform.

Rip shoots the Marines gathered around the fire a salute. A haggard looking man sighs, places his meal on a small, stone table and stands.

"At ease," the man says. "Name and rank?"

"Sergeant Ripley Vross."

The man nods, gaze shifting to Gerty. She straightens. "Corporal Gertrude Cortez, Sir."

Finally, he squints at Alyx. "And you?"

"Dr. Alyx Wick."

The man sighs again, shakes his head. "Hunt should've kept you folks at home. There's nothing special here." He clears his throat. "I'm Captain Miles Rogers." He points at a scrawny man with a bush of messy red hair. "This is Private Maxwell Connors." He nods at a dismal woman with a shaved head. "That's Lieutenant Amelia Verity. And over there," he points at another woman, this one with black hair, glowering at Alyx, "that's Sergeant Katy Crowe."

Gerty and Rip quickly salute each other. Though none return the same respect. To Alyx, all four soldiers appear on the verge of some mental breakdown. They're all covered in dirt. Their eyes are bloodshot and weary. There's a strong sense of tension biting the air around the four. After a moment, they all return to their meager meals and continue staring into the fire.

Captain Rogers turns to Rip. "Hunt didn't send a full platoon?"

"Company A, Sir. Elite Marine Unit. There was only six of us. Lieutenant Hannah Briggs is back at our cruiser repairing it."

Rogers nods solemnly. "Company A? Where's Captain Row?"

Rip draws in a slow breath, blows it out. "He's dead, Sir." Rip pats his pack. "Ashes are in a containment tube, along with Sergeant Fern Williams. They both perished in the tunnels."

Rogers shakes his head. "Those tunnels. We lost four of our own in them."

"How'd you guys get through the really narrow spot?" Gerty asks.

The Captain frowns. "Really tight spot?"

Sully clears his throat. "I do believe we arrived in the city through different tunnels. Ours were wide, though our presence awakened the creatures living in the dirt floor."

"Yeah," Gerty says. "Not so different than what happened to Fern. Were there holes in the walls too?"

Sully shakes his head. "No holes, dear."

Everyone falls silent for a few moments. One of those awkward silences where no one can think of a good thing to say.

Then Sully takes Alyx by the arm and leads her away from the Marines. He takes her to what might have been a home at one time but now is a crumbling ruin. The ceiling has caved in on one side and the inside appears to have been destroyed. Only...

Alyx brushes her fingertips over a few deep grooves in the stone walls. And the more she inspects, the more of the same grooves she finds. So many in such a small room.

She glances at Sully over her shoulder as he places the cylinder on the floor and taps the top of it. A dark purple light consumes the room. She should've realized what the thing in his hand was right away. A dark light. One of the trinkets Sully loved to use. It eliminates all the shadows, bright, scarlet splatter marks are revealed. The dark light shows what is invisible to the naked eye.

"What..." She's at a loss for words.

"So far," Sully says, walking to one of the splatter marks. "These aren't in any other buildings besides those on this street."

"Shit, Sully, what the hell happened here? Looks like a massacre."

He turns to her, winks. "You're probably not too far off in that assumption, kiddo."

She once more touches the deep grooves. "And these...?"

"What do they look like to you, Alyx?"

Four deep gashes in the stone. In some places it's two or three, but here, on this wall, it's littered with the four. So many amongst all the splatters.

"Claw marks," she says through numb lips.

"That they are. So, what do think might have happened here?"

She eyes the splatters, the claw marks, the brokenness of the place, then faces Sully. "An assassination?"

Sully smiles. "More like a purge, dear."

"A purge?"

"That's my theory, anyway. Why are these found *only* in the homes of this derelict street? Why is everyone gone? Where'd they go? My theory is this, the most powerful in their society ordered a purge of the poorest among them. They let loose some kind of beast that devoured the poor." His face is grim in the dark purple light. "Then they all gathered in that large structure out there."

Alyx shakes her head. "But why? Why would they gather there? Mass suicide?"

To this, Sully shrugs. "We won't know until we find a way inside. But collecting all the data and evidence of this city as I can, it makes sense they migrated there. With the lack of bodies or bones, this is the only thing that might have happened to them. However, this is just a theory of mine."

"Sounds plausible," Alyx says, frowning at the scarlet splatters all over the walls. "You're right, though, we need to get in that structure to know for sure. And maybe the artifact Hunt wants is around here somewhere."

"To be honest," Sully says, "I don't think the artifact truly exists. Nothing here points to it."

Alyx nods. "I figured as much. So, what are we going to do? I mean, we can get out of here and haul ass back home."

Sully strokes his white beard for a moment, thinking, then says, "There might be something here to find, though. Maybe not the artifact General Hunt seeks, but something close. In a house on the main street there were pages on a table indicating a special object shaped like a pentagon in cylinder form. This might very well be what is called a healing tool. If I interpreted the drawings and text correctly, it might enlarge a planet two-fold."

Alyx smiles. "I missed you, Sully."

He chuckles, embraces her in a firm hug, and steps back to look at her. "And I you, dear. Been too long."

"Yeah. I'm sorry about that."

"Oh, never be sorry, Alyx. Never. I've been following your findings over the years."

She gulps. "You…you have?"

"I can't say I agree with your methods, but I do admire your drive to discover and find the unfindable. Even if you are considered a pirate to some, I admire you still."

Her heart swells a little. To hear the one she admires say he admires her somehow makes everything bad she's done for the sake of money moot.

"Thank you," she manages.

"Now," Sully says. "How about you help me find a way into that structure?"

Her smile feels too big and silly on her face, but, "Yes. Let's do this."

It's been a long time since she got a chance to work with her mentor and she can't wait to get started.

"We shall," Sully says. "First, have you eaten yet?"

"No. Been pretty much on the run since we arrived. Maybe about twenty-four hours by now."

He chuckles. "Well, there are a few of those dreadful packaged meals the Marines brought with them. Taste like carboard and dishcloths, but it will fill the stomach just fine."

"I'll give it a whirl."

They joined the Marines by the fire and Sully handed her one of the packaged meals.

She didn't know what to expect when they returned to the Marines, but laughter hadn't been on her mind.

And yet, here they are, laughing and cracking jokes. Even angsty Gerty is all smiles. This does Alyx's heart good. The girl has a beautiful smile and she needs to do more of it. Here she has other women to talk to that share her struggles. Even if the others are a bit older, they all went through the same shit daily. The whole equality thing, even after centuries, hasn't quite stuck. Maybe a little, but for the most part, the men can still be assholes with a woman among their ranks. It's like they just can't fathom a woman by their side kicking more ass than they are.

It's more than stupid. More than ignorance. It's a goddamn tragedy because women have proven time and again they can be more badass than some men.

It's a battle that might very well last forever.

Sully clears off a chair and tells her to sit. She does, and rips open the packaged meal.

Years ago, the military ended their MRE run. Proven not to be beneficial to sustain energy or nutrition, the meals were redesigned. Crackers and such were replaced by tubes of protein paste and vitamin pastes.

Now, as Alyx looks at the thing, there's only one item that resembles actual food, the pretzels. She chows down on these first, savoring their saltiness. Sully hands her a canteen and she takes a few deep swallows of cool water. Then she tears open the protein paste tube and empties the entire thing into her mouth. She chews a few times, then swallows. The taste isn't horrible, for the most part. Like stale peanut butter. There are worse things. She finishes with the meal and tosses the trash into the fire where it melts into nothingness.

"Tasty?" Alyx glances to her right, finding the dark haired woman—Katy Crowe?—giving her a withering look and looming over her.

"Um," Alyx says. "Not really."

"That's our food."

The tension is like steel cables twisting in the air. Cables getting tighter and tighter. Sooner or later, they're going to snap and then…

Alyx stands. "Didn't see your name on it." Her hand drifts toward the revolver.

"That's quite enough, Ms. Crowe," Sully says, stepping between the two women. "Dr. Wick is my most trusted protégé."

"Doesn't give her the right to eat our food. We could be stranded down here for *months*."

Alyx can't help but laugh. "Not if I can help it."

Sully is shoved aside and a blade is pressing against Alyx's throat faster than she has time to react. All she can do is suck in a sharp breath.

Crowe's foul breath puffs into Alyx's face. "Oh, you're a real badass, aren't you? A real smart lady." Crowe grins, revealing yellow teeth. "Tell me, badass smart lady, have you ever killed anything?"

"Crowe," Rogers shouts. "That's enough."

Before Crowe can step away, Alyx wrenches the knife out of her hand, sidesteps and taps the blade against the woman's deeply bronzed cheekbone.

She smiles. "I've killed more things than you can imagine, *lady*. Do not *fuck* with me."

Crowe's eyes are wide. Her breathing pauses.

Alyx presses the revolver into the woman's stomach. "Now, we can work together down here and find a way out. We can survive and honor those who have fallen, or I can kill you right now. It's your choice."

She shoves Crowe away and hands the knife back to the woman.

Sully pats Alyx's shoulder. "I need to talk with you a moment, Dr. Wick."

Crowe steps away, sheaths her knife, and returns to the meager group of Marines.

Sully leads her to the street. "There's something you must understand about these soldiers, Alyx."

"That they're assholes?"

"No. They are actually a very kind group, considering. What they don't like are outsiders, like you. They're skeptical. They don't trust you. You need to understand that before interacting with them further."

Alyx sighs, then nods. "Understood."

"And do not antagonize them. They are loyal to each other. Not us."

"Okay. Sorry. I just don't take kindly to someone talking to me like that."

Sully chuckles. "I know, dear. But try and play nice, okay?"

"Alright, Sully. Alright." She points at the giant shadow of the Coliseum structure. "Ready to tackle that thing now?"

The old man smiles. This time she can see it through the beard, even in the flickering glow of the firelight. "Absolutely. We need to inform the Marines. Perhaps they will join us."

"Gerty and Rip are good people, they'll come along."

"So are the rest of Company 3, actually. They're just different personalities that tend to clash from time to time."

"Well, let's see what happens then."

Together, they approach the Marines sitting around the fire.

Gerty shoots Alyx a smile. "There she is." She nudges Amelia. "This lady saved us from some shit."

"Thought you lost two?" Crowe spouts.

"We did. But Alyx here, she warned us before anything happened. She was watching after us, but no one listened."

"And we should have," Rip adds.

The other four Marines stare at her and once more she wants to step back into the shadows. She hates being the center of attention.

"What's with the hat?" Crowe asks. "No one wears those hats."

"It was my father's," Alyx says. "Brings me luck."

Sully steps in front of everyone, garnering everyone's attention. "Dr. Wick and I have a plan. One that might offer rewards."

"You better not be talking about finding a way into that giant whatever it is over there," Rogers says. "Because that's a waste of time, my friend."

"Not necessarily. Every structure has some kind of entrance. We just need to look."

"Dude," Crowe says. "We've been around that damn thing over and over. There's no way in."

"Ah," Sully says and grips Alyx's shoulder. "But I have an extra mind here to help. One of the best."

Crowe humphs and looks away.

"In any case, I believe time is of an essence. Dr. Wick and I can go alone, if you all need rest."

"No," Rogers says, standing. "You go, we all go. You're lucky you snuck away the last time."

"I didn't go far, but yes, please, if you want to help, that would be fantastic, Captain."

Rogers gives a single nod and rouses the Marines. Gerty and Rip immediately stand beside Alyx. Once everyone is ready, Sully gestures for them to go.

No one moves until Rogers says, "Move out."

They make their way to the structure in silence.

FOURTEEN

The Coliseum structure, to Alyx, appears to be at least one hundred feet tall and about three hundred feet wide. The thing is massive. Beyond massive. How they'll find an entrance, she doesn't know. It'll take years if every inch is to be inspected.

But Sully says, "Remember when we were on the planet Gul and we were looking for the Velician Coin?"

Alyx thinks a moment, then nods. Another insane exploration that yielded one of their biggest finds. But she's not sure what Sully means. What about that planet?

"Remember the old rock wall that went around the entire island where the coin rested?"

She blinks. "Yes."

He touches the solid stone structure. "We couldn't get through it. Couldn't climb over it because of the venomous vines. So, what did we do? I honestly cannot remember."

"We, um…we found a weak stone in the wall. Then found the gate."

Sully claps her on the shoulder. "Correct. So, if everything has a weak spot, where would this thing's weak spot be? This is what I want you to consider while searching."

She wants to hug him, realizing every little exploration was actually a lesson for her. He was teaching her even though she never knew it.

As the Marines gather around them, Sully says, "Every structure has a weak spot. I want all of you to look for these. If you think you find a weak spot, I want you all to mark it by any means necessary for further inspection."

"How will we know what a weak spot looks like?" Gerty gestures at the structure. "I mean, it's pretty solid, people."

Sully says, "A crack. A place where the color of the stone is off from the rest, even just a little bit. Keep an eye out for the slightest flaw."

"Also," Alyx interjects. "Don't just look at the walls themselves, but everything close to it. An out of place rock pile, or anything that feels odd to you. Mark anything that feels different."

Rogers steps forward, narrow face lined with a frown. "And why do we want to get in there, again? You think the artifact might be inside? Because if this is just a fool's mission for two nerds, then I'm putting a stop to it right now."

"I assure you, Captain," Sully says. "It is important to see what's behind these walls. Could be exactly what we're looking for."

"But you're not sure?" Crowe nudges Rogers. "This is bullshit. We should be finding a way out of here."

"There's a way out the way Gerty, Rip and I came," Alyx says.

"And I believe we can leave the same way we entered as well," Sully adds.

"Through that horror show?" Crowe laughs humorlessly. "Yeah, no thanks. We lost too many through that fucking tunnel."

Ever the patient one, Sully says, "Now that we know the creatures are there, we can be prepared."

Crowe shakes her head and turns away from him and the group, visibly sulking. Sully isn't her commanding officer and Alyx is sure she's having a hard time taking orders from the man. But still, Rogers doesn't object. He stands there, gun slung over his shoulder, lights trained on the wall.

"Okay," Alyx says. "Let's see what we can see."

"Fuck you," Crowe mutters as she joins Amelia. Alyx watches them walk away. Despite the attitude, both women appear to be inspecting the wall closely.

"I want you with me," Sully says to Alyx.

"Where she goes," Gerty says, "I go."

Rip, Connors, and Rogers glance at each other, shrug almost comically and focus on the wall.

Leading Gerty and Alyx around the wall, Sully says, "This could be the finding of a lifetime, so be vigilant, dears."

Leaning close to Alyx, Gerty whispers, "So he's your mentor?"

"Yep."

"Makes sense, he's definitely smarter than you." Gerty chuckles, patting Alyx's shoulder.

Alyx laughs. She can't help it. The joke wasn't exactly that funny, but it feels good to laugh.

Then they're all inspecting the wall and whatever stands out around the wall. And as they do, Alyx's heart sinks a bit because the wall is nearly perfect. No flaws. No cracks. Nothing remotely close to the structure besides...

"Wait," she says, crouching in front of a softball sized black rock.

When everything else around is gray stone, the black sticks out. And there's nothing else like it nearby, as far as she can tell. She touches the black rock, glances at the wall. It's about two feet from the structure.

Sully crouches opposite of her, cool gaze on her. "Do you find this of great significance, or shall we mark it and keep moving?"

"I...I don't know. Hold on."

She runs her fingers around the rock, dust swirling away from her. She brushes more of the dust away and—

"Found it."

Tracing around the bottom of the rock is a paper-thin crevasse.

Alyx stands, smiles at Sully. "Worth a shot, anyway."

Sully, however appears a bit dubious as his gaze drifts from her to the rock. Though he doesn't say anything.

"Um, it's just a rock, Alyx," Gerty says.

"Maybe. But..." She stomps onto the black rock as hard as she can.

It slams into the ground. Dust plumes in all directions. A hollow *thunk*, and then a line shoots up the wall directly in front of the depressed rock.

Sully places a hand on her shoulder. "Your skills are surpassing mine, dear. Well done."

The line in the wall begins to widen. The ground quakes. A nearby building collapses from the vibration sending a wave of dust over them. It happens so fast, Alyx forgets to secure her mask. Then again, no one else does either.

Once the dust clears, a large section of the structure opens up. The space is wide enough to fit a cruiser or two through easily. Beyond this opening lies another wall, though this one is darkness. Seemingly so thick not even Alyx or Gerty's light penetrate. At least not from the outside.

A dry, musty odor washes out of the opening.

"Prepare yourselves for what awaits," Sully says. He turns to Gerty. "Get the others, dear. We'll wait here for your return."

"You better," Gerty says and runs off to gather the other Marines.

Once she's out of earshot, Alyx cocks an eyebrow at Sully. "What do you mean, 'prepare', Sully? Is there something inside I should know about?"

"If I knew what was inside this gargantuan, I wouldn't be worried. But, do you smell that? That musty, almost meaty stench? Tell me, what smells like that after time?"

It doesn't take her long. "A corpse."

Sully sighs. "Prepare yourself, dear."

Alyx opens her mouth to ask what it is he's not sharing when the Marines come running.

"The nerd's figured it out," Crowe says and claps Alyx on the back hard enough to hurt.

Alyx grits her teeth, refraining (barely) from punching the woman in the face.

Sully stands in front of the opening. "I want you all to stop a moment. What is inside this structure, it might not be pleasant. I want you all to keep your wits about you as we explore. Stay close to each other."

"Yes, Dad," Amelia says.

Rogers nods toward the wall of darkness inside. "We have a high-density lamp with us. Could use it in there."

"That would be terrific, Captain. Thank you."

Rogers hurries away to get the lamp. Alyx isn't so sure it'll do much good, but it's worth a shot.

While everyone is chatting amongst themselves, Alyx notices Sully step away, talking into a slender, silver gadget. Never in all the years she knew him has the man used a voice recorder. But then again, he is older. His memories might not be what they once were. Still…

She looks away when he stops talking into the thing and drops it into the inside pocket of his jacket. Maybe it's an old age thing, but she plans on asking him about it later once they're alone.

A moment later, the Captain rushes in with the portable lamp. He sets it up just inside the opening.

"This, ladies and gentlemen, might be what makes our losses worth it," Sully says and turns to the opening just as Rogers flips on the high-density light.

And for a moment, Alyx is blind, even standing behind the thing. It's this bright. She squints against the glare, shielding her eyes with her hand until, finally, her vision adjusts. Compared to the shoulder lights on their gear, this thing is a brilliant glare. Like a spot-light, only fanning out wide to eliminate any shadow within distance, which is about three hundred feet.

Then Gerty says, "Oh…oh shit…"

As Alyx steps around the lamp all the blood freezes in her veins. Tiny lumps spread over her skin and a breath snags in her throat like a fish bone. She coughs, clearing the sensation and beside her, Sully places a gentle hand on her shoulder.

"No matter how much we prepare, we can never hold back our horror at the sight of death."

She manages to tear her gaze from the scene to the man. "You were right. They gathered here."

He nods solemnly.

Alyx faces the scene, unable to look away now. Her sight fixes on what lay before her.

The dead sprawl as far as the light touches. Corpses hanging over railings like old cloths. Corpses piled onto the stone floor, hands reaching toward the cavern ceiling, frozen into grasping claws. To Alyx, they are much like those ancient Egyptian mummies from Earth's past. Minus the wrappings, of course. Their clothing, she supposes serves as their death shrouds. It clings to them in dusty tatters. Each and every one. Being fairly sealed off, the dead didn't so much decompose, but wither like mummies.

"What happened to them?" Rip asks, face drawn.

"That," Alyx says, "is what we're going to find out."

"I don't really care what happened. I—wait, do you notice something about them?" Crowe points at the nearest corpse. "Why is this one missing a head?"

Alyx frowns, moves closer to the dead. She kneels, inspecting another dried-out body. The smell is dank, not pleasant, yet tolerable. This one, its back is ripped wide open and one of its arms has been chewed off. Or at least, that's the way it appears. She stares at the exposed, gray bones sticking out of the back and shoots a concerned look at Sully. "They were all murdered."

But the man shakes his head. "Not murdered. Sacrificed."

"Sacrificed to *what*?" Gerty asks, eyes all wide. "Are you *seeing* this? They've been torn apart."

Sully doesn't respond to her and instead steps through the tangle of corpses toward what Alyx assumes was a pyramid while on the platform above the city. Standing in front of it now, as it looms over her, she realizes it's not a pyramid, but an octagon with a flat top. Like a symmetrical plateau. It ends a good fifty feet from the top of the walls surrounding it.

Sully makes his way toward a wide opening in the octagon, or whatever it really is.

"Should we follow him?" Gerty whispers in Alyx's ear. "I mean, this is kinda messed up."

"I trust him," Alyx says and carefully works her way through the tangled dead to catch up with Sully.

The closer she gets, the more she realizes he's talking to himself.

Or is he…?

She reminds herself about the voice recorder, or whatever it really was, Sully spoke into moment ago.

Alyx can't tell if that's what he's doing now, but it's the only thing that makes sense right now.

Sully never talked to himself as far as she knew.

She shoves it out of her mind as they approach the opening to the octagon building. Here Sully stops and glances at her. His face is full of excitement.

"This is a shrine."

"A shrine?" Alyx surveys the building. "To what, though? And why is everyone torn apart? You said a mass sacrifice, but to what and *by* what? Sully, if we're in danger you need to—"

"Oh, I'm quite sure the danger has passed, dear. But I feel what we seek is inside this."

"How do you know, Sully?" Alyx spares a few glances around, finding nothing but the twisted dead. "You haven't inspected the area." This is how Sully used to work. He inspected the area around a location, finding clues. It took time. He never fully assumed anything.

"No need to inspect," Sully says. "These bodies won't yield clues. All we have is this." He waves at the opening of the octagon building.

Alyx frowns and lets him see it.

Sully sighs. "Look, dear, my methods are less tedious these days. I've learned to get to it rather than inspecting for so long. People have grown impatient."

"Since when have you thought about what people think?"

"Since I needed to pay for my daughter's treatments." And when Alyx's eyes widen, he nods. "She has ALS, my little Miranda. Her treatments will cure her, but they must remain constant. A single break could mean death for her. Yes, I'm working for more money than I used to. Yes, my methods have changed, but all I think about is her. And what kind of father would I be to let my child wither away without at least *trying* to save her?"

"Oh, Sully," Alyx manages. "I'm so sorry, I didn't know."

"And let's keep it that way. Best you don't know. And if asked, pretend I never told you."

"Huh? What?" Gerty says as she steps beside Alyx.

Sully smiles. "Nerd talk, dear."

Gerty rolls her eyes. "Figures. So, what are we going to do now? If you think I'm going in that thing you're nuttybars."

"You can wait outside," Alyx says, still trying to really process what Sully told her about his daughter.

There is a cure for ALS now, but it takes many extensive treatments for it to take hold.

"Sweet," Gerty says. "I get to hang with all the dead people."

"Either that or the unknown inside," Alyx says. "Your choice."

A long sigh blows out of the girl. "Where you go, I go."

Rip moves to Gerty's side. "And where she goes, so do I."

Alyx smiles at them. It warms her heart to know, after everything, they're still there for her. The news from Sully weighs heavily on her as they face the wide doorway into the octagon. She knew he had a daughter, and by now she's somewhere in her mid-twenties. Pretty much grown. Ah, but ALS is a withering death. And if you have the money, you can save loved ones from it. If you don't however, well…

It all comes down to money, as it always does. As it has for centuries. Money is the devil's tool, but no one can live without it. Even the hermit needs some form of currency from time to time.

And as Sully takes the lead entering the dark belly of the octagon, she wonders how much Hunt is paying him for this little venture. And if it's enough.

FIFTEEN

Inside, it's large enough for her and Sully and all the Marines to fit and walk as a group.

Gerty and Rip flank Alyx. Behind them, Roger, Crowe and Amelia follow. Private Connors was ordered to remain outside and keep watch. A task the young Marine appeared unsure of. But with Rogers's order, he has no choice.

Alyx wishes the boy would've disobeyed the order. Leaving someone behind isn't what she does. Then again, she has no choice in the matter either. She doesn't have to take orders from Rogers, but she does have to respect the chain of command with the Marines.

Their boots clomp heavily on the smooth stone floor, echoing down the hall. Inside the octagon, there is no dust. No dirt. And there's no musty smell. In here, it's like stepping into a grotto. The air is cool on her sweaty skin and smells faintly of minerals. Along the walls of the hall they tread, spaced every six feet or so, are burnt out torches. She thinks about lighting one of these and later dismisses the idea. They all have their shoulder lamps. The lights are ten times better than any ordinary torch and direct the illumination outward so they can see clearly ahead for a good twenty yards.

No one speaks as the hall gives way to a massive, round chamber. Lining the walls are large ovals made of stone which protrude from the otherwise smooth walls. There are no descriptions or glyphs etched into, or around them.

But these are the last thing anyone focuses on. What draws the attention is the single, white stone altar standing at the center of the room like some kind of obscure lynchpin.

Sully strokes his white beard, frowning at the white altar. On top of the flat surface, there's a metal cage. Inside the cage rests an object Alyx can't quite make out from where she stands. Her gaze drifts away from the altar, searching for visual signs of a trap. Because, apparently, traps like to find her.

As far as she can tell, there are no seams running through the stone floor, or the ceiling. Beside every oval protrusion stands an entrance to what might be tunnels or archways to other chambers. Eight in all. Other than all this, there's nothing to her that indicates a possible trap. Though, in her experience, she's stumbled upon many illusions. What appears as a wall can actually be something far more sinister.

Still, there's an odd sensation prickling over her skin and she doesn't know why.

"Dr. Wick," Sully says. "Accompany me, will you?"

"I don't know about this," Alyx says. "Something doesn't feel right."

"Only way to find out, dear, is to find out."

Alyx sighs. "You haven't encountered many traps, have you?"

Sully chuckles and she follows him to the white altar. The Marines, even Gerty and Rip remain behind. Which is for the best. Too many people around one thing sometimes ends up badly.

"Remember, keep your wits about you," Sully says.

"Right."

Inside the cage is the artifact Sully described to her earlier. In the shape of a long octagon. It rests on the altar, about a foot long or so, all shiny black like onyx. The very thing to increase the size of a planet and make it habitable. Yet, looking at it now, she wonders how something so insignificant and small can do those things. Makes no sense. Unless there's magic involved. Which is possible. Magic, like science, go hand in hand throughout the galaxies.

God knows she has faced her share of magical objects throughout the years.

A pain in the ass, every one of them.

Sully and Alyx stop about two feet from the artifact.

"This isn't what General Hunt wants," Sully says, "but it's what she's going to get. I already signed the contract so she has to pay me what I agreed to regardless."

"She's gonna be pissed, though."

"Yes," Sully says and bends, inspecting the metal cage around the octagon artifact. "Cannot be helped."

Closer now, Alyx carefully steps around the altar. There's nothing, as far as she can tell, indicating a trap. Everything appears solid. Even the cage is embedded into the flat surface of the altar.

"I think," Sully says, "we can cut away this cage without incident."

"One of the Marines have a laser cutter that you know of? Because I sure as hell don't. Not even bolt cutters."

Sully humphs. "All those years, you never did come fully prepared." He brings out a small, black gun with the needle-like muzzle.

"Well excuse me all to hell," Alyx says, smiling.

He winks and places the narrow muzzle against one of the bars of the metal cage. About eight inches above the artifact. "Might want to step away for a moment, dear."

Alyx moves away from the cage and altar and Sully presses the laser cutter's trigger. Sparks spray, then the laser slices through the metal as easy as a sharp knife through bread. Sully cuts through each bar cleanly. The top of the cage clanks to the stone floor.

The Marines had moved forward a few feet. Gerty catches Alyx's eye. She shrugs, as if asking what's going on. Alyx shrugs back, conveying she's not sure. Or at least that's how she hopes Gerty takes it. The girl doesn't show whether or not she does and steps away from the others. Rip notices and follows suit.

Rogers, Crowe and Amelia gape on without a word or expression. Their faces are so blank, Alyx realizes. Like living statues. So different from Gerty and Rip. Company 3 aren't the elite like Gerty and Rip, and yet, they're the ones showing no emotion whatsoever. To Alyx, this doesn't make much sense. Then again, the remaining soldiers of Company 3 have been through a lot. Company A, Gerty and Rip's platoon, has suffered greatly too, but they are seasoned. Even if Gerty is younger, she's probably seen more shit than Crowe or Amelia. The girl is tough.

"Okay," Sully says, pocketing the laser cutter. "Let's get this thing and get out of here."

"Sounds good," Alyx says.

The old man is reaching into the open cage when a sharp beep sounds. His eyes widen, hand frozen above the cage. Then Sully visibly shivers.

"You alright?" Alyx asks.

Sully blinks. "It's…just my heart equalizer. Give me a moment."

She frowns at the old man, but doesn't say anything. A heart equalizer means he's had a heart attack. It means he's at serious risk for another one. It also means with him freezing like that his heart rate is too high.

"Just take it easy," Alyx says. "I'll get it, Sully. Just relax a bit."

Sully shakes his head, sweat trickling down his wrinkly face. "No. Just give me a moment."

"Your heartrate is too high. The equalizer is tripping. You need to relax."

After a moment, the old man sighs and withdraws his hand from the cage. He steps away, as another fit of shivers racks his body. Alyx smiles, but he does not return it. He's too caught up in whatever pain he's suffering at the moment. Rogers steps beside him and gives Alyx a nod, as if telling her to go ahead.

Alyx draws in a slow breath, blows it out, and reaches into the open cage. Her hand wraps around the cylinder octagon and carefully lifts it out. She holds the artifact up in front of her, showing Sully. This is his show. This thing is why he's here. A job to get enough money to save his daughter.

Sully finally smiles. "Now…let us get—"

The floor trembles, throwing him off balance enough for Rogers to grab him before he falls. Dust sifts from the ceiling and small cracks snake across its smooth surface. Then, all at once, the trembling stops. For a moment, no one speaks, then Alyx hurries around the altar to the others.

"Time to go," she says, taking hold of Sully's arm and leading him toward the main exit.

"There are no traps," Sully mutters.

"I'm cursed," Alyx says, trying to make light of the situation. "Traps always find me."

To this Sully merely snorts as she leads him toward the exit.

No more than six feet away, a stone door drops down, sealing off the exit.

"Shit," Alyx says and turns with Sully to the nearest doorway next to one of the oval protrusions.

She's almost to the doorway when a loud cracking sound echoes through the chamber. She stops, glances around.

"The shit was that?" Gerty asks as her and Rip join up with Alyx and Sully.

The other three Marines gather around. Rogers's face is hard when he says, "You brought us into a fucking trap." He's not looking at Sully. No. His glare is directed at Alyx.

"Back off," Rip says.

Rogers shoots the big man a withering look. "Is that how you address a commanding officer, Sergeant?"

Rip grunts. "*My* commanding officer is dead. I'm in charge of my platoon now."

"I still outrank you."

"Does it look like I give a shit?" Rip lifts an eyebrow. "Sir."

"Oh great," Gerty says. "We're all stuck in a pissing contest now."

"Sergeant," Roger says. "Once we arrive back home, prepare yourself for a court-martial."

Rip chuckles. "Yeah, good luck with that, man."

Rogers surges forward, rifle muzzle jamming under Rip's chin. "Look, you son of a bi—"

Another loud crackling sound interrupts Rogers.

This time, Alyx is able to locate the source. Then again, she's not sure how anyone couldn't. She stuffs the artifact in her pack.

Across from them, on the other side of the chamber, one of the oval protrusions has two long cracks zig-zagging down its center. Top to bottom.

"We need to get out of here," Alyx says.

Now everyone sees the cracks.

"What the hell?" Crowe starts across the room and Amelia pulls her back.

Rogers, seeing the cracks now, steps away from Rip. To Alyx, he looks like he's about to blow chunks everywhere. That greenish, sick look crawls over his face. One she's seen before on other people. Where fear and stress congeal into a horrifying stew and you just can't take it anymore.

The Captain, however, swallows it down and says, "Move out."

Everyone hurries to the doorway.

Another tremble shakes the floor.

"Go," Alyx says helping Sully through the doorway.

The Marines follow close behind as more crackling noises sound. Alyx turns just enough to see into the main chamber, and all the air whooshes out of her like a hard punch to the gut. An ashen claw emerges from the oval protrusion across the chamber, peeling away the stone. She watches the shards of stone shatter on the floor and shouts, "Move! Now!"

Helping Sully along, they all enter a smaller chamber.

The moment they do, another stone door drops, sealing them inside.

Crowe roars, beating her fists on the solid door.

"Get a grip," Gerty says.

Crowe spins on the girl, teeth visibly gritting. "What did you say to me? What did you say, you little *bitch*?" The woman unsheathes a knife as she storms toward Gerty.

In a single, fluid motion, Rip disarms Crowe and tosses the knife aside. He looms over her. A giant. "Leave her be."

Crowe, however, does not move for at least a full minute. Her glare burns into Rip. Then, finally, she turns away to stand with Amelia and Rogers. It's clear now, to Alyx, how truly divided they all are right now. There's no respect from either side.

Sully, trying to keep his breathing slow, says, "Traps."

Alyx can't help but laugh a little. "They're assholes, aren't they?"

He manages a wheezy chuckle. She sits Sully on the floor, leaning him against a smooth, gray wall and faces the small chamber they stand in now. There are no other exits besides the sealed off doorway. It's just a round room with an orb hanging from the middle of the ceiling. She stares at the orb for a long time. It must mean something. Who builds a room with an orb protruding from the ceiling like this anyway? Right now, nothing makes sense except for the fact that they are trapped in this chamber and whatever was breaking out of the stone in the large chamber, it's out there now.

Out there, just waiting for them to open the door...

SIXTEEN

"Hey," Gerty says. She steps beside Alyx. "How's it going?"

"Shitty," Alyx says, straightening from what she thought was a seam near the far wall but is only a crack. "You?"

"Well, Crowe and Amelia are assholes, but other than that, Rip and I have been thinking about sleeping in shifts just in case."

Alyx lifts an eyebrow. "You think we'll be in this chamber that long? Such little faith, my child." She grins.

"Yeah, yeah. I said just in case. I don't trust them. Even Rogers feels off."

"Agreed."

Gerty sighs and waves a hand at Sully, who slumps against the wall not far away. "Is he okay?"

"He has a heart equalizer." Alyx shakes her head. "Hopefully it stabilizes him soon."

"And if it doesn't?"

"Then…we're in trouble because if anyone can get us out of here, it's him."

Gerty smiles. "You know what I think?"

"What?"

"I think if anyone can get us out of here, it's *you*." She walks away before Alyx can respond.

She watches Gerty join Rip and they stand near Sully.

Alyx fetches a breath, too heavy to be a sigh, and returns to inspecting the chamber. The other three Marines, Rogers, Crowe and Amelia, they stand near the stone door, whispering amongst themselves.

After checking out the entire chamber, her attention is once more drawn to the orb hanging from the ceiling. It's too high for her to reach, but…

"Rip," she says.

The big man straightens, frowns.

She waves him over.

He glances at Gerty. She nods. Then he hurries over.

"What's up?"

Alyx points at the orb. "Can you reach that?"

Rip says, "Oh, I think so." He stretches and his hand palms the orb like a basketball. "And what do you want me to do with it?"

"Can you turn it, or push it? Anything?"

He grunts, pushing up as much as he can. The orb doesn't budge. He tries using both hands. Still, nothing.

"Try pushing," Alyx says.

Rip pushes. Nothing.

"Try again," Alyx says.

"It's not working, Alyx," he says through gritted teeth.

Nonetheless, he shoves up on the orb harder and—

The dusts sifts into Rip's face. He lets go of the orb and spins away, wiping dust out of his eyes and growling deep in his throat.

Slowly, the orb lifts into the ceiling. A loud hissing noise erupts around the round object. The chamber fills with a vile stench. Something Alyx can't place no matter how much she tries. An alien stink that churns her stomach.

"It's gas," Crowe shouts. "You bitch. You killed us!"

"It's not...gas," Sully says leaning against Gerty for support. He must've gotten to his feet while Alyx was focused on the orb. "It's air. Old, pent up air." His face is so pale, eyelids droopy. "It's...releasing pressure for...for..."

He slumps against Gerty. The girl gives Alyx a worried look. All big eyes and parted lips.

"Jesus Christ," Amelia says. "Spit it out, old man."

"Shut up," Alyx says, shooting the woman a glare. "He's ill."

Amelia throws up her arms in exaggerated exasperation. "Of course he is. Now, of all times, he's ill and can't fucking talk."

"It's releasing pressure for an internal pulley system," Alyx says, not really knowing if that's what Sully meant at all. Just guessing. And yet, as she listens, somewhere behind the stone there are clicks and squeaks. The sound of a pressurized machine, perhaps.

Rogers and the other two shift away from the stone door.

Sully, breathing heavily, places a hand on Alyx's shoulder. His eyes are all glassy looking. Not a good sign. "This...is a killing chamber, A-Alyx."

"Wait, what?" Gerty's wide-eyed stare burns into Alyx.

Alyx faces everyone. "Listen up. This is a killing chamber. Get your guns ready."

"A killing chamber for *what*?" Crowe asks.

"For whatever came out of the oval stone back in the chamber. And when that door opens it'll charge in here looking for its meal."

Everyone sort of stops and stares at Alyx.

She turns away from them, again, hating the attention. But what other choice do they have now? Sully is dying. His heart equalizer isn't helping. And with him incapacitated, that leaves her to figure out how to escape this place. Not a huge deal, but she's never had to work with Marines before. Mercenaries, yes. Actual by the book soldiers? Nope.

There's something a little intimidating about being in such staunch company. Besides Gerty and Rip, of course.

Rogers, Crowe, and Amelia, however...

Within the walls, floor and ceiling, the sound of grinding stones and squeaky pulleys.

Alyx arms trickles of sweat from her face and draws her revolver. She reloads the cylinder, slipping fresh bullets into the chambers. Then she waits.

Gerty and Rip rest Sully against a wall and stand on either side of her while the other three Marines take a position just a few feet to the right of the door. Rip lowers to one knee, rifle aimed at the door as it shudders.

"Hold," Rogers says. "As soon as it enters, light'em up."

Alyx can almost feel Gerty's eyeroll.

The stone door shudders. Dust and bits of rock fall to the floor.

Behind her, Sully is saying something. Or trying to. But she's so focused on the door she doesn't pay much attention. His wheezing voice rambles on and she can't hear his words. She needs all her focus on the door. Because as soon as it opens shit will get—

A new sound rumbles to her right. A grinding, clicking sound. The floor quakes.

Alyx blinks, draws in a breath, and risks a glance to the right just as a section of the wall drops into the floor. Her eyes widen. Her heart stutters. And out of the darkness emerges a monster. She opens her mouth, meaning to shout a warning, but all she can manage is a low whine. Every muscle in her body feels as wobbly and unsubstantial as gelatin.

The monster steps through the doorway, vulpine head lowered, red eyes fixed on Alyx. Leathery ears fold back. Its muzzle peels away, revealing long, pointy teeth. By all accounts, it resembles a wolf from Earth. Only much larger and hairless. Its skin is utterly white, as if dipped in bleach. Its massive shoulders hunch. Large claws click on the stone floor.

Finally, her shock breaks. "On the right!"

Everyone lifts their head, blinking in obvious confusion.

Alyx swings herself to the right and pulls the trigger before she has the thing fully in her sights.

Ears ringing, she fires again.

There's a few seconds of utter silence as the gun smoke clears.

The creature isn't there.

Alyx frowns, gaze slipping over the room. But it couldn't have gotten by her. It couldn't have—

"Heads up," Gerty shouts, rifle bursting to life.

Crawling on the ceiling, littered with smoldering holes, the beast roars. Alyx aims the revolver, narrows on the wolfish head, squeezes the trigger. A tidal wave of black consumes her world. And somewhere in all that black, a meaty thump.

She stumbles away, wiping the hot blood from her face. It's like wiping away tar. Thick and sticky.

"*Shit*," someone says. "You see that thing?" Sounds like a woman, but for a moment, Alyx can't see anything.

When she finally clears the blood away from her eyes, Gerty is pulling her toward something. The new doorway.

"C'mon, Alyx. We gotta *move*."

"Sully?"

"Rip has him. Now c'mon!"

Alyx shakes out of her disorientation and follows Gerty out of the chamber. They enter a wide tunnel. Behind her Rip carries, literally carries, Sully in his arms. And behind Rip, Rogers, Crowe and Amelia follow. She pulls away from Gerty's hold to look into the chamber.

On the floor lay a limp, pale figure. A large pool of black blood surrounds it like a tarry moat.

Then Gerty tugs on her arm. "We need to *move*, Alyx."

She allows herself to be pulled away and is soon running with the team. Sully's head lolls as Rip runs with him in his arms. Eyes shut, as limp as the dead thing in the chamber back there, Sully already looks dead. Alyx swallows down her worry and tries to think. Tries to get a grip on the situation.

For one thing...why are they running?

Nothing is chasing them and from what she's noticing, they're going deeper into the octagon temple. Or whatever this thing is. A sacrificial temple? A damn slaughter house?

She slows her pace and shouts, "Wait. Everyone stop a minute."

They don't listen. Fear, or something even more primal, drives them like rats through a maze. As if a snake is stalking the maze, the Marines run and run without direction.

"Stop," she shouts. "Something isn't right." She slows to a jog, breathing heavily as a stitch stabs into her just below the armpit.

Gerty and Rip stop and turn to her. Judging by their wide eyes and tense postures they're on the verge of some freak out. Seeing this with trained, elite soldiers scares her a bit.

"We...have to keep moving," Gerty manages between breaths.

"All we're doing is going deeper inside this place. Feels like..." Alyx pauses. "Feels like cattle being driven to slaughter."

Gerty and Rip exchange a frown.

Ahead, the other three Marines continue on without pause, their boots clapping on the smooth stone.

She doesn't even try to call them back and realizes now why they were the ones to survive the attacks in the tunnels. They ran. They left the others in their platoon behind and ran for their lives. Just like now. Cowards, all of them.

All but Gerty and Rip. And they're barely holding it together right now.

Alyx checks on Sully. His pulse is weak and his skin feels cold and clammy to her touch. He shivers now and again and mumbles things she can't understand.

"So," Gerty says. "What do we do?"

"We passed a few narrow passages. Offshoots, I believe might bring us back to the main chamber."

"Why the hell would we want to go back there?" Rip asks. "It's sealed off. We're trapped in here."

Alyx shakes her head. "There has to be a release lever or something to open the door." She thinks about this. "Unless it's only located outside. The black rock."

"So, our only hope is that ginger soldier out there? Um...whatever his name is." Gerty looks away, obviously trying to remember the boy's name.

"Connors," Alyx says.

"Huh?"

Alyx smiles. "His name is Connors."

Gerty's eyes light up. "Oh, yeah."

"But yes," Alyx says. "If there's no internal release, he's our only hope, I think."

"You don't think there might be a backway out?" Rip asks.

She ponders this a moment. "Maybe. There's usually a few exits in temples, but this is different. This is more like a slaughter house. A sacrificial building." She cocks a thumb over her shoulder. "That creature is supposed to feed on whoever gets put in here. It's also like a giant puzzle. If the sacrifices can figure it out, they go free. But that's just a theory."

"Makes sense with that orb in the room back there," Rip says.

Alyx nods. "And I think if we can find more releases like that, we'll get out of here."

Gerty gives her a wan smile. "Well, here goes nothing."

They backtrack to the first passageway Alyx noticed in a blur the first time. It stretches out into complete darkness.

Gerty laughs nervously. "I'm getting sick of these things."

"You'll do fine. Remember, think of your favorite open space."

The girl nods, though her face is sullen. Alyx knows the last thing she wants are more tight spaces, but if this is a way out, then it's a way out. She can almost see the gears turning in Gerty's head right now. Weighing pros and cons.

"Whatever we're doing, let's get it done," Rip says. "He's starting to get heavy."

Without another word, Alyx leads them into the narrow passageway.

About ten feet from the opening, the floor trembles and a stone door slams down, shutting them in.

"You gotta be fucking kidding me," Gerty says.

Alyx sighs, turns to face the long darkness ahead and says, "Traps. I hate traps."

SEVENTEEN

All around them, the building groans. A low, ominous sound that slips under the skin like slivers of ice.

"What *is* that?" Gerty asks.

"The place is waking up," Alyx says.

"Waking up? It's not alive, it's a goddamn *building*."

Alyx doesn't respond as her mind churns with thoughts. Maybe it's not alive, but it's definitely a working machine. An old machine, yet one still very much functional. And like any machine, it has an off switch. It has a way to stop it. The trick is finding the off switch before they all die in here of dehydration and starvation. And that switch just might very well be in the main chamber. Maybe she's wrong, but checking it off the list will help move her in another direction. Process of elimination. Or something.

She's just happy the batteries on their shoulder lamps haven't expired yet. Without light, this venture would be much slower. Military grade batteries are wonderful things.

The walls of the passageway are covered in strange glyphs.

If she had more time, maybe she'd try to decipher them.

But she doesn't have time. All that matters is getting out of this place.

"Hold up," Rip says. His face is sheened with sweat and he's breathing heavily. "I need to set him down for a minute."

Alyx and Gerty help lower Sully to the floor.

The man mutters, "The...gates."

"Gates?" Alyx props him up against the wall and kneels in front of him. "What gates, Sully?"

But the old man's head droops. His face tenses, as if in pain. His body shudders. A muffled, yet shrill beep sounds from inside his chest. A thin whine from within. A sound she's never heard before but can assume it's not good. And the way Sully slouches against the wall, she really doesn't have to assume much at all.

With a trembling hand, she reaches out and presses her fingertips on Sully's neck, right over the artery. Nothing.

She draws her hand back quick, as if touching something extremely hot...or cold.

"No," she whispers, tears welling in her eyes. Her vision blurs, and someone, maybe Gerty places their hands on her shoulders.

Alyx shakes her head. "No. He can't be gone. Not now." She slaps Sully across his pale face. The sound is sharp, loud and brimming with sorrow. "Wake up! Wake up, damn you! Your daughter needs you!" She slaps him again and again. "Wake up, Sully, you hear me? Wake up!"

Hot tears cascade down her cheeks and she goes to slap the man again. A large hand catches her by the wrist, and when she looks up, she sees Rip's face swimming in tears.

"He's gone," Rip says in a low, gentle tone.

"N-No," Alyx says. "Check him. He's alive."

Gerty steps over Alyx, crouches, and places her fingers over the same artery as Alyx had. And when the girl doesn't move for almost a minute, hope springs inside Alyx. Then Gerty looks at her sullenly and shakes her head.

"He's gone, hun."

Alyx bites back a sob. She wants to hit him again. If he knew of his condition, then why the hell did he accept such a dangerous mission? If he needed money so badly, why hadn't he gotten ahold of her? Surely he'd been keeping tabs. All he had to do was reach out and she would've given him the money he needed.

But would you have? Really? The voice inside sounds too much like the emotionless pirate side of her. And she hates it. *No. You wanna know what I think? I think you would've bought him coffee, talked the old days and sent him packing without a dime.*

She hates it, because it's the truth. She'd been so hung up on money and retiring to her own private island on some lazy planet she would've had a few laughs with the man. Reminisced a bit, then they'd go their separate ways.

God, when did she become such an asshole?

"Come on," Rip says, helping her to her feet. He turns her to him, large hands firmly on her shoulders. "I'll incinerate him to go with the others, if you want."

She spares a final look at Sully. Her mentor. Her good friend. The one who taught her more than just exploration and archeology. He's the man who taught her how to remain human.

"No," she says. "He'd want to stay here."

"He would?" Gerty lifts an eyebrow.

Alyx pulls away from Rip and kneels in front of Sully. She rests a hand on his sunken chest. "He never wanted a funeral. He told me once, that if he ever died while working, to leave him where he lay." She wipes away a stray tear. "So he can continue the adventure in a new life." She pats his chest and something metallic glimmers from the inner pocket of his jacket.

Blinking, she brings the cylinder object out of his pocket. She turns it over in her hands.

"What's that?" Rip asks.

"A voice recorder, I think," Alyx says and slips it into the pocket of her pants.

She stands, sighs and smiles. "Happy venturing, Sully."

Then she walks away, leaving Gerty and Rip to gape at her as she goes.

She can't linger around the old man anymore. Sully wouldn't want that. He—

A loud roar crashes down the passageway.

"The fuck was that?" Gerty asks.

Alyx, upholstering her revolver, says, "Something hungry."

"I thought it was just one," Rip says.

"Me too," Alyx says, pointing her gun at the darkness.

But after a few moments of nothing, she holsters the gun and turns to her friends. "Probably the building and all the pressure going on."

"Wait, is thing going to explode?" Gerty's gaze shifts to the ceiling.

"No," Alyx says. "It's like a pressurized machine."

"I see. Can we get the hell out of here now?"

Alyx smiles. "Let's go."

They hurry down the passageway, leaving Sullivan White's body where it lies.

EIGHTEEN

The passageway breaks off into smaller tunnels. Too small for anyone to fit through comfortably, until they come to a T-intersection.

"It's like the damn tunnels all over again," Gerty spouts.

Alyx checks out both passageways. They're the same in width and height. Neither one appears better than the other.

Shit.

She stares at the left passage for a long time. In any other situation, this one will lead them back to the main chamber. But…seeing how this place is a machine of sorts, then…

"We go right," she says.

"You sure?" Rip asks. "Left makes more sense."

"It does. But everything in this place is rearranged. Nothing ever moves, yet it does. It uses illusions, I think. Like the tunnels."

"So everything is the opposite?" Rip asks.

"Something like that. But I'm not sure."

She enters the passage on the right. For as far as the shoulder lights shine, the passageway is clear.

They walk for what feels like forever. Hours, probably. The passage appears to have no end. As they walk, Gerty and Rip chat quietly. Something about transferring to a different base.

Alyx brings out the voice recorder. It's about four inches long with a narrow screen embedded in it. A mesh section toward the top indicates the microphone. Toward the bottom is another mesh section. The speaker.

On the screen, there are three options. Play. Record. Transmit.

Frowning, she touches Play. A list pops up.

She saw Sully talking into it twice and decides to play the second to last recording.

Soon, Sully's weary voice floats out of the speaker.

"The dead await us on the other side of these walls. It's the only explanation which makes sense. My esteemed protégé, Dr. Alyx Wick, is assisting me on this discovery. I am glad to have her here, for her talents exceed my own. I just hope the Marines of Company 3 will respect her more. It saddens me to see her struggle with them. If they only knew how great she truly is then maybe they'd listen to her. I now stand before the opening to the sacrificial area of the city and expect death to greet us as I know no matter how much I prepare them, the others won't be ready for the sight. Sullivan White, out."

Tears threaten to fill her eyes again and Alyx forces them back. Barely.

"Wow," Gerty says. "He was like a dad, wasn't he?"

Alyx sniffles, smiles. "Y-Yeah. He taught me everything I know."

Beside her now, Gerty nudges her lightly. "Not everything. Besides, you rock."

Alyx shakes her head, chuckling. Praise is something she's not used to.

"And we're here for you through it all," Rip adds.

"Thank you," Alyx says.

Who knew she'd make friends out of Marines? They were just people, but strictly trained people. People made to fight and kill. People made without emotion. How Rip and Gerty retained their emotions is beyond Alyx.

She plays the last recording.

"Thanks to Dr. Alyx Wick's intuition, we have gained access to the inner building, for which I can only assume is made for sacrifices. We were in a large chamber lined with oval protrusions. Next to each is the entry to a passageway. Like tunnels, I suppose. And when Dr. Wick lifted the artifact from the altar, we found ourselves in a smaller chamber. Something was breaking free of one of the protrusions. I fear there is more than meets the eye in this place. I just hope Dr. Wick feels it too. I hope, because my heart equalizer is stalling. I'm not sure how much longer I have left. I want all listening to this to know Dr. Alyx Wick is the answer to all explorations."

Alyx blinks away more tears.

He knew something wasn't right the moment they stepped into the smaller chamber. He knew and he tried to warn her. The muttering he was doing. He was trying to tell her to watch out. Trying to get her attention, because he knew the place was built in a way to surprise and slaughter those trapped inside.

She's about to pocket the recorder when she notices a new message under the transmit option.

Her thumb hovers over this for a moment, then she touches it.

"Dr. White, this is Vilas. How are things down there? The rescue team has arrived. I am stalling. Hopefully you retrieve the artifact soon. I'm not sure how long I can keep them distracted. If they continue pushing, I may have to kill them. I know you said you didn't want any more death, but…"

Vilas's voice cuts off into static.

Alyx opens her mouth, closes it, not sure what to think or say. She sets the recorder in her pack.

"The shit?" Gerty pushes around Alyx to face her. "He was working with *Vilas*?"

Alyx's hand brushes along something cold inside the pack. Her eyes widen and she brings out the octagonal artifact. "I guess he was. But it must have been for a good reason. Sully didn't have a bad bone in his body." She holds up the artifact. "But without this, Vilas won't leave us here."

"Okay, only none of that made sense," Gerty says, rolling her eyes. "He was *working* with that bastard up there. *Nothing* about that feels right."

"And Vilas still has Lance," Rip says.

"That's if Lance isn't already dead," Gerty nearly shouts.

"He's not," Alyx says, returning the artifact to her pack. "Now let's get out of here."

The passageway veers to the left. The curve getting sharper and sharper.

A scream echoes through the passageway. She stops, trying to see around the curve. A series of short-burst gunfire trails the scream. Then...silence.

"If you tell me that was pressure build-up, I'm gonna punch you in the face," Gerty says.

"Definitely not pressure build-up," Alyx says. "Keep moving."

They round the curve and find themselves about ten feet from a stone door.

"Great," Gerty says. "It's like being stuck in a tube."

"Shh," Alyx says and carefully approaches the door.

Her sight slips over every spot on the floor, shifts to the walls, the ceiling, until finally resting on the door itself. There's no sign of any way to open the door. At least, nothing visible quite yet. Alyx traces her fingertips along the sides of the door.

"Finding anything?" Gerty asks.

Alyx chokes back her irritation. Having her full focus is important. She needs to connect with places. Needs the quiet. People talking interrupts the connection. It—

A small piece of the wall to the right of the door flakes off, revealing a red gem. Something similar to a ruby only littered with blue flecks.

"Everyone stand back. Not sure what's behind this door," Alyx says, then presses the red gem. It shakes under her finger, sinks into the wall, and disappears.

She steps away, heart whip-cracking against her ribs. But nothing more happens. Where the gem used to be is now but a hole in the wall.

"Huh," Gery says. "Well, that was—"

The door drops into the floor. Dust plumes, cutting off their sight into whatever awaits beyond.

Alyx draws her revolver, just in case and—

"Hey," Gery says. "It's where we started. You did it, Alyx!"

Alyx waves a hand to clear the dust away from her face and smiles. The main chamber sprawls before her. Her sight glides over the white altar, the partial metal cage on the floor, and she can't help but think about Sully. Dear, kind Sully who only wanted to get enough money to save his daughter from the awfulness of ALS. Sully who—

Then her gaze falls on the broken oval. The section of wall the beast broke out of. A translucent substance drips out of the crater. The thing this entire temple, or whatever, was built for, no doubt. Well, at least it was only one and...

But her sight drifts to the next oval protrusion. Like the one beside it, it's broken wide open. More of that translucent substance oozes out onto the floor. She can't help thinking about eggs. And the stink as they enter the chamber is something like spoiled milk. Milk months old opened for the first time. A sour reek.

Alyx turns slowly, taking in the scene. All of the oval protrusions are broken open. All eight of them.

"Um," Gerty says. "Weren't those other ones solid before?"

"Yeah."

"This isn't good, is it?"

"Nope."

Alyx hurries to the main door. It's much wider than the others, but she checks out possible ways to open it from the inside. There's no orb in the ceiling. Likewise, there's no red gem on either side of the door. She even has Rip brush along the top, above the door, just to make sure. Nothing.

She drops to her hands and knees, inspecting the floor, but again, there's nothing. And apparently Private Connors hasn't either noticed, or figured out how to open the door.

"Shit," Rip says. "So, what now?"

Alyx stands, shakes her head and looks around. The large chamber is what Sully would call an empty cell. Meaning, there's absolutely no puzzle to solve. A dead end. Or a way to distract...

Her eyes widen.

But she's too late. The creature skids into the chamber from one of the passageways. It slams into the altar, rebounds and faces Alyx, Gerty and Rip. Its wolf-like head lowers, muzzle peeling away from long teeth. It's about the size of a male lion. Drool drips onto the stone floor. A low growl rumbles through the chamber. Its white skin ripples as it slowly moves toward them.

Rip steps in front of the women and open fires.

Alyx steps aside, points her revolver at the thing and shoots. She hits it twice before it darts to the right, hops onto the altar like a grotesque gargoyle, and leaps at them. Gerty joins Rip, pumping laser sonic rounds into the beast. Black blood mists the air as the thing's momentum carries it directly into Rip before he can move away.

Both beast and man slam to the floor. Still alive, it clamps its maw onto his shoulder. Rip roars in mingled pain and what Alyx can only assume is rage. He slams the muzzle of his rifle into the creature's temple and pulls the trigger. Its head explodes into an inkblot, splattering Rip and Gerty.

"Ugh," Gerty says. "Bastard."

Rip shoves the creature off him, rolls onto his stomach and gains his feet. He wobbles a moment, then says, "Ouch."

His right shoulder bleeds badly. Alyx checks her pack for a first-aid kit, and finds a sealed bag of gauze and various quick-fix remedies. She tears the bag open with her teeth and goes to help Rip with his shoulder wound when a loud roar echoes through the chamber.

She manages a half turn when something heavy crashes into her back. She lands hard onto the stone floor as the thing on top of her buries its claws into her sides. She screams as hot agony laces through her body.

Then, all at once, the pain lessens. There's a short burst of gunfire, a squeal. Then silence.

She rolls onto her side just as Gerty puts a laser sonic bullet into another creature's head.

Alyx sits up, grimacing at the pain stabbing into her sides. Thanks to the tactical gear under her jacket, the claws didn't go too deep. Or at least, she hopes not. She cuts away Rip's shoulder gear and finds an angry looking bite mark. His skin is torn, but once again, thanks to the gear, the wound isn't as bad as it could've been. She patches him up as best as she can and sighs.

"Sorry, guys. This isn't the way out."

"Kinda figured that out after you didn't find anything," Gerty says.

Alyx manages a thin smile. "Right. Anyway, the way out might be through any of these passageways, except for the one we already took."

"I need a damn bomb," Rip says. "Blow a hole in the door."

"Do you have a bomb?" Alyx grins.

Rip chuckles, wincing from the pain in his shoulder. "I wish. Doubt a grenade will do anything as thick as these walls are."

"Yeah, a grenade will leave, maybe, a scuffed surface."

"Well, looks like we're doing some more walking." Rip tips her a wink and moves toward the center of the chamber.

"You alright?" Gerty asks. The girl's expression is full concern.

"Yeah," Alyx says. "I think so. It didn't get me too deep. Thank you."

Gerty smiles. "No need. We're a team."

Even though it hurts to walk, Alyx pats Gerty's shoulder and makes her way to the center of the chamber with Rip.

"I have some painkillers in the bag if you need them," she tells Rip.

But the big man shakes his head. "I'll live."

She nods. "I know. Just making sure."

Rip favors her with a smile and she smiles back.

After a moment, Rip faces her. "So, I'm at a loss. Which one should we take?"

Alyx eyes all seven passageways, six, minus the one they returned to the chamber through. So, six passages. If they had more time and resources, she'd try out each. But since they only have what water and food Gerty and Rip carry, then their situation is a bit more dire. She needs to figure out which passage is the right one. Which one will lead them to a way out. But then again, how the hell is she supposed to figure that out? There's no way to know for sure which passageway is the right one.

Despite all her knowledge, this chamber boasts absolutely nothing to go on.

So, six passageways. Three creatures dead, five more still stalking the darkness. And considering the possibility that each creature hunts their own passage...

The last one came through the passageway directly across from the small chamber they were trapped in. Or did it come from the one nearby? Everything happened so fast, she can't remember for sure. And what about the one that attacked her? Which passage had that one come from?

She's not sure if either Rip or Gerty saw, but...

Her gaze drops to the floor and, of *course*.

One of the beasts did indeed emerge from the passage directly across from the small chamber they were stuck in for a while. The long swath of claw marks leading to the altar proves this much. Her eyes narrow as she moves to the next passageway, sight slipping over the floor. Nothing from the opening near the claw marks. She steps from one passage to the other, bypassing the closed off one they reentered the chamber from.

Then she stops at the passageway a few feet away from the small chamber. The marks here are faint, but they're there. Signs of the beast perhaps stalking, then scratching off as it sprinted at her.

This leaves two relatively safe passages. Only problem with these, however, all comes back to what Sully taught her about taking the lesser road. Both passageways might be safe, but will they lead them to a way out, or trap them?

She's pondering this when Rip says, "My shoulder burns like hell."

Alyx hurries over to him as Gerty lifts the gauze bandage. The thing drips with a yellowish liquid. Then Gerty gasps. She shoots a worried look at Alyx, lifting the bandage higher. The big man's shoulder has doubled in size, swollen, oozing with infection. Dark streaks squiggle down the man's arm and snake toward his throat.

Alyx rummages through the first-aid bag, but doesn't find any form of antibiotics. Not even a salve. Just pain killers.

Rip takes in the sight of his shoulder and grimaces. "Well, shit. That's not good."

Gerty sighs. "We'll fix ya up, hun. No worries."

Chuckling humorlessly, Rip shakes his head. "Whatever was in that thing's bite, it's in me now." His face stills as his gaze drifts to one of the dead creatures. A gaze full of darkness. "I...I feel it. It's like a bunch of spiders crawling under my skin."

"What?" Alyx frowns. "What are you saying?"

His eyes, so glossy dark, roll in her direction. "You have to kill me."

Gerty shoves him. "Stop being dramatic, asshole. It's just infected. We'll get you out of here and—"

"I'm infected, alright," Rip says. "It's spreading. Its's..." His darkening eyes lower.

Alyx draws her revolver, points it at the big man. "Okay, Rip. Okay."

Gerty kicks the gun out of Alyx's hand. It clatters on the stone floor.

"Like, *hell*," Gerty says, pushes Alyx back and faces Rip full on. "What do you mean it's *spreading*? You weren't bitten by a fucking *zombie*." Her voice trembles and all Alyx can do is look away.

Rip releases a long breath, inhales shakily, and says, "Maybe its bite is similar. I feel it worming through me, kiddo. I—I can't even think."

"Maybe it's nothing," Gerty says. "You're just overacting."

No matter how much Alyx wants to tell her about the time back on Earth when a mutant bear bit one of her assistants and he about died. Only he didn't die, he turned into kind of werebear. A beast far worse than the thing that created him. She wants to tell Gerty how, if she had killed that man after he'd been bitten eight lives could've been saved before she blew his head off.

She can tell her all of that, but chooses to keep silent. None of it will help the girl either way.

Still, there might be a chance Rip is mistaken too. What he's feeling just might be progressive infection. Deadly, but not altering. Besides, if this is true, then why isn't she feeling anything? She had claws stabbed into her, after all. Unless…unless that's not how it works here. Maybe what it takes is a real bite.

But…

Alyx says, "Let's keep moving. Rip, I'm going to change your bandage, give you a painkiller, and you're coming with us."

The big man visibly shivers, shakes his head. "No. You don't…you don't understand. Something is…inside me."

"Nothing but an infection," Alyx says and Gerty gives her a look she can only assume is perplexed. "You'll see. Once we get out and get some antibodies in you, everything will be fine."

Rip's red rimmed, darkening eyes blink at her and she knows without a doubt what's going on.

"No," Rip says, upholsters his sidearm and rams the muzzle into his mouth.

"Rip," Gerty shouts moving to take the gun away from the man and—

Crack.

The back of Rip's head explodes into bits of skull, blood and gray matter. His body jitters for a second or two, then collapses to the floor.

"No!" Gerty drops to her knees beside the dead man. She yanks the gun from his hand and tosses it aside.

"Gerty," Alyx says, but the girl flips her off.

Sobbing, Gerty touches Rip's face. "Thank you for everything, old man." She sniffles, and says, "You're the dad I should've had."

Alyx turns to the passageways, worried another creature will attack from the shadows.

She doesn't even look as shifting noises and clinks sound behind her.

Then, at her side, Gerty says, "I'm gonna incinerate him and bring him with us."

Alyx nods, not trusting herself to speak.

A moment later there's a flash of heat and the stench of charred flesh.

NINTEEN

They walk down a passageway Alyx randomly chose. Both women beaten and torn. Broken. Their souls splattered in darkness and sorrow. Two women staring straight ahead awaiting death to come storming out of the shadows and devour them both.

And yet, the passage leads ever onward. Only silence greets their progress.

Gerty carries Rip's pack and his flashgun. As an added form of protection, she also carries his rifle. No matter how much Alyx insisted she carry the rifle, Gerty refused, saying Alyx isn't a soldier and the rifle is a soldier's weapon. The girl has this far off gaze Alyx doesn't much care for, but knows nothing she can say will help. Gerty is grieving. She doesn't want to let go.

These things happen.

So, Alyx lets the girl grieve. She remains quiet, trying to think of a way out of this horrible place.

She's not sure how long they've been walking when Gerty says, "Sorry. He was just the only dad figure I ever really knew."

"No need to apologize," Alyx says. "I get it. But can I tell you something? Something I learned over the years?"

"Sure."

Alyx stops, places a hand on Gerty's shoulder. "Use it. Use that rage and pain and turn it into something unstoppable."

Gerty grins. "Oh, I plan to."

Alyx smiles. "Good. Now, let's kick some ass and find a way out of here. What do you say?"

"I say…" Gerty lifts her rifle. "*Oorah.*"

Patting the girl's shoulder, Alyx nods and leads the way deeper into darkness.

They're walking for what feels like forever, when a low growl sounds somewhere behind them.

Gerty stops, spins around. "C'mon, you bastard."

Alyx says, "Not here. Let's see what's up ahead."

"We've been walking for a long time and this thing hasn't even made any turns. It's never going to end." Gerty lifts her rifle. "I say we go hunting."

Another growl echoes, this time sounding much closer.

"We do that and we'll get all mixed up." Alyx sighs heavily. "Look, I feel your pain. I've felt it before. But going on a hunt right now is the worst thing we can do. They're distracting us. That's how they wear their prey out. Distractions and disorientation."

"You think Rogers, Crowe and Amelia are dead?"

The question is so random it takes Alyx a moment to grasp it. When she does, she says, "I don't know." It's the truth.

Now the growling is so close, the creature might as well be on top of them.

"It's too late to run," Gerty says. "Better draw that primitive sidearm of yours. It's almost here."

Alyx pulls out her revolver, glances behind them, then back in the direction of the growling. "Aim for the head."

"It's dead right now," the girl whispers. "It just doesn't know it yet."

The growling stops, leaving a long void of eerie silence.

Alyx's heart thuds heavily against the walls of her chest as she squints at the darkness her shoulder lights can't quite touch.

Stealthy scratching noises above her. Flakes of stone drift in front of her.

Her eyes widen. "It's above us."

Gerty sucks in a sharp breath, then says, "On the count of two, shoot it." She waits a second, then counts, "One. Two. Now!"

Alyx steps backward, pointing her gun at the ceiling as Gerty opens fire. The beast squeals as bullets pummel into its body. Black blood splashes the walls, pours onto the floor as it jitters back and forth.

Alyx aims at its vulpine head, squeezes the trigger. The left side of its head bursts into a mess of bone and black goo.

"Move," Alyx shouts as the creature's claws unlock from the ceiling.

Gerty stumbles backward just in time to avoid being crushed by the beast. Its pale body thuds to the floor. Black blood splatters everywhere, even finding Alyx's pants.

Pumping a few more shots into the beast, Gerty roars.

Once the girl is finished, Alyx says, "Let's go."

They hurry on down the passageway without a word, picking up their pace until both women are jogging. The urge to get out of this place grows stronger with very step.

Alyx is about to call for a break when the passage ends at a four-way intersection. She opens her mouth to tell Gerty to go left when a woman crashes into her from the darkness to the right. Both go down, but the other woman scrambles to her feet.

"Get out," the woman says, pacing and scratching her head at the intersection.

Alyx frowns. "Crowe?"

The woman Marine paces, not saying anything. Her hair is in disarray. Blood, human blood cakes her gaping face. Her eyes dart without really seeing anything. A coppery stench wavers off her.

"Getoutgetoutgetout," Crowe whispers.

"Jesus," Gerty says. "What's wrong with her?"

But Alyx can guess. Rogers and Amelia are dead. The blood covering Crowe is evidence enough. She stands and grabs Crowe by the shoulders.

"Hey, look at me."

Crowe does everything but look at Alyx.

Alyx slaps the woman. Hard. Right across the face. And still, Crowe doesn't acknowledge her. The woman has fallen completely off the nutwagon.

"What's wrong with her?" Gerty asks again.

"She's losing her mind," Alyx says. "Too much trauma."

"Shit, she was crazy before now anyway."

Alyx tries to ignore this, but can't help believing it. Crowe had been an ass to her, but crazy? Maybe, but probably not. Well, not as far gone as Gerty thinks.

Crowe was going through a power struggle earlier, sure, but she wasn't exactly crazy.

Alyx leads Crowe toward one of the passages and presses her against a wall. "Crowe. Where's Rogers?"

The woman shakes her head, dark hair flying in every direction. She struggles against Alyx's hold. She smells like sweat, dirt, and something like onions. But there's something else slithering just under all of these odors. Something sour. The stench of fear, perhaps. God knows Alyx has smelled it before and probably had the same stench about her too over the years.

"Crowe, hun," she says. "I need you to be strong now." She positions the woman's head so Crowe is staring directly at her. "Can you do that for me? Can you be strong?"

The poor woman blinks, then, after a moment nods. Her gaze never leaves Alyx. "Dead. Rogers. A-Amelia. It got them."

Nodding, Alyx gently squeezes the woman's shoulders. "Let's get out of here, what do you say?"

Crowe's mouth opens and closes like a fish out of water. Finally, she says, "Amelia...she's different now. Not her. She's..."

Alyx cocks her head. "What do you mean?"

"She's bad now. Tainted. It bit her. She's...oh god, we need to get out!"

Alyx sighs. "Yes. Let's go."

Crowe shivers, nods and says, "Okay. I'm okay. Sorry. Just...I'm okay."

Gerty says, "You said Amelia was bit? What happened?"

Crowe spins on the girl, smacks the gun away and slams Gerty up against the wall, hand on her throat. "She fucking turned. What the hell do you think happened? She's something else now. She's a monster."

Alyx shoves Crowe away from Gerty. "Knock it off." Her focus is fully on Crowe. "If we're going to make it out of here alive I need you to—"

A shrill howl echoes up one of the passages. Alyx isn't sure which one. Crowe sucks in a sharp breath through her teeth, as if being slapped. She fights against Alyx, winning and goes sprinting down one of the passages.

"Shit," Gerty says. "What the hell do we do now? I say we let her go. She's gone nuttybars."

"Don't the Marines train you not to leave anyone behind?"

Gerty slips Alyx a snarl. "Yes. Damn it." She glares into the passage Crowe ran into. "Let's get her."

And even though Alyx wants nothing more than to figure a way out of this place, she leads the way in finding the terrified Marine.

Another shrill howl echoes.

"I don't even know where it's coming from," Gerty says.

"It's close," Alyx says, changing her pace to a jog. "That's all we need to know."

Eventually, they find Crowe curled up against a wall sobbing. When Alyx tries to get her to her feet, the woman screams and thrashes. It's the first time Alyx notices the woman doesn't have a gun. Not even her sidearm.

She's defenseless.

"Come on," Alyx says, trying to get Crowe to her feet. "We need to move."

But the woman shrieks, curls up and refuses to move.

Alyx glances at Gerty. The girl lowers her head.

Alyx kneels in front of Crowe. "If you don't stand up and move right now, you'll be stuck down here alone with those things without a weapon. You'll die and destroy everything Rogers and Amelia died for. They died for the sake of humanity. What honor will you receive by just sitting here?"

But Crowe cowers, curls more into herself and refuses to move.

"There's no use," Gerty says. "We can't—"

The howl rises behind them a few seconds before something slams into Gerty, knocking her off her feet. She goes down with a heavy thump, manages a gasp, then it's on top of her. Most of its face is split open and what was once human is no longer. Skin hangs in ragged flaps as a lizard-like snout snaps from where a face should've been. What's left of the hair dangles in greasy strings. And judging by its length, Alyx can assume this is Amelia. Or used to be.

The thing perched on Gerty is ghost-white, emaciated, and sprouting small, thorn-like spikes all over its naked body. Its red eyes narrow on Alyx. Its lizard maw opens, revealing rows of sharp teeth, then snaps shut. Its hands are no longer hands, but ashen claws hooking into Gerty's back.

The girl struggles to get her sidearm, but the thing must be too heavy. She can't wiggle enough to pull her arms free, which are pinned under her.

Crowe wails, scrambling away from the scene before Alyx can grab her.

"Shoot it," Gerty shouts, face laced with pain.

Without further hesitation, Alyx points her revolver at the creature and fires. The gunblast once more deafens her. Most of the monster's head explodes in a mess of blood and bone, splattering onto the wall beside it. It twitches violently for a moment, then falls onto Gerty.

"Get this fucking thing off me," the girl screams. "Get it *off*!"

Alyx kicks the dead thing off Gerty and helps her to her feet. The girl is visibly shivering, obviously hurt, but otherwise okay. There's a tiny scrape on her chin. She whirls, kicks the dead creature that used to be Amelia.

"Goddamn fucking monsters always jumping me!" Gerty kicks it again and faces Alyx. "Where's Crowe?"

"She ran off."

Gerty closes her eyes, takes a few slow breaths and says, "Do you think this tunnel or whatever might lead to a way out?"

Alyx shrugs. "I don't know."

"Because, if not, I say we go back and try a different one."

"This might be the way out," Alyx says. "Or it might not be. I just don't know."

"Well, you're the expert, right?" Gerty squares up in front of Alyx. "Be the fucking expert."

"Without a map or anything to go on, I'm doing my best, Gerty. Now back off."

The Marine's face pinches in what Alyx supposes is contempt. She raises one of the rifles. "You lead. I'll watch our backs." Her eyes soften a bit. "Get us out of here, please."

Alyx opens her mouth to tell Gerty she'll do her best, when a bunch of scratching noises echo up the passageway. This is soon followed by more than a few low growls.

"Shit," Alyx says.

Gerty half turns just as four of the pale beasts emerge from the darkness and sprint at them. Long maws open wide, teeth gleaming, Alyx knows her and Gerty are already dead.

The young Marine opens fire on them. And even over the rapid rattling of the rifle, Alyx can hear her roar.

Aiming for their heads, Alyx manages to pick off one before realizing it's more than four of them racing up the corridor. There are dozens.

She grabs Gerty by the arm. "Run!"

The girl, apparently realizing they are very outnumbered, the passageway choked by the growling, and gnashing teeth and sharp claws, stops shooting and together both women run down the narrow corridor.

Behind them, gaining…death follows.

TWENTY

The passageway turns this way and that, with no end in sight and Alyx has enough time to hate herself for choosing to go after Crowe rather than figure out the right corridor when they find themselves in a larger chamber very similar to the first one.

But…

"It's a gate," Alyx shouts, pointing at a wide area across from them. Sweat trickles down the small of her back and she can't help but laugh. "Sully was right. There's a gate."

"Yay," Gerty says, turning back to the passageway, rifle ready as the growls and scratching claws echo into the chamber. "Now figure a way to shut this door and get us out, lady. Because…damn."

Alyx returns to the doorway leading into the passage. She feels around for a moment, and…

"There's no way to close the door."

"*What*? It's just like the other ones. Where's that red gem or whatever?" Gerty begins checking around too, but Alyx knows it's no use.

This is the end of the line. Or meant to be, for every sacrifice. The final standoff. If the person can kill the beasts, they are set free. If not…

This theory becomes more and more reality as she kicks through a heap of bones toward the gate. "They're concentrated in the passageway. It's like a bottleneck."

"Huh?" Gerty says, glancing over her shoulder.

"Hold them off as long as you can. Don't let them in here where they can spread out."

Gerty grunts, and points the rifle at the open doorway. "Just get that gate open."

Alyx falls silent as she searches for anything odd. But there are no out of place stones, nor levers, not even an orb. The passage Gerty stands in front of is the only way in or out, save for the gate. A large, metal thing with thick bars buried deep into stone.

The only thing that sticks out is a concaved octagonal shape carved into the wall a few feet from the gate.

She kicks through another small heap of bones to get to the shape in the wall. Dust billows, and settles. She touches the shape, frowning.

Gerty's rifle bursts to life, making Alyx jump.

Okay, now her time is really limited. Alyx's lips form a thin, pink line on her sweaty face. Because, despite it all, Gerty will need to either reload or switch guns. And all it takes is a second for those creatures to spill through and flood the chamber. Just a second, and they're both dead.

The shape is an octagon. Just like the building. Just like everything else she's encountered. Just like...

Alyx's breath snags in her throat. Her heart slams into her ribs and she fumbles in her pack to bring out the artifact. Of course. It's not just a thing to behold, or grow planets, but it's also a *key*. Somehow, Sully knew this. He tried to tell her as agony stole over him. He tried, and she hadn't paid much attention.

Now, though...

Between a barrage of gun blasts, Gerty shouts, "So opening that gate would be pretty damn amazing right about now."

Alyx places her pack on the floor, grabs the artifact and brings it out. Wiping sweat from her face, she steps closer to the wall with the octagonal shape carved into it.

Through the squealing and rumbling gunshots and Gerty's roars, Alyx slams the artifact into the concaved shape. A hollow click, more felt than heard, sounds.

Alyx almost laughs to herself, a bit of relief spilling through her.

Over her shoulder she yells, "When I tell you, stop shooting and run for the gate."

Between blasts, Gerty manages, "Well hurry it up already."

Alyx draws in a breath, blows it out, and turns the artifact. A gritty sound, like churning gravel finds her ears. She keeps turning until finally something in the wall clinks and she can turn the artifact no more. The floor quakes. Shards of stone fall from the ceiling and shatter at her feet. She moves away from the wall, keeping a close eye on the gate. If it doesn't move, they're dead. Simple as that.

She waits and Gerty roars and shoots her rifle at the things struggling to get through the passageway into the chamber. The ones still alive, they dig their way through the bodies. Through their dead. Ripping and splashing black blood everywhere. Gerty picks each one off quickly, but how much ammo does the Marine have left? Is she still using her rifle, or Rip's? Alyx doesn't know and there's no time to worry about it. Either the gate goes up, or it's good-bye Dead World.

And the gate remains shut. The floor still shakes, the walls crack, but the gate doesn't move at all.

"Did you fall asleep on me?"

Alyx kicks a skull. It bursts into dusty pieces. "No. The gate isn't moving."

"What?"

"I said, the gate isn't moving."

Gerty takes out two creatures trying to wriggle out of the bottom of the pile of dead bodies. "Then you better figure it out. Running low on ammo over here."

"Whose gun are you using?"

"Rip's. Any longer and I'll need to use the flashgun."

Alyx blinks. "Wait, what?"

"Huh?" Gerty pumps a few rounds into a beast clawing through the right side.

Alyx snaps her fingers. The idea of simply melting through the gate takes up most of her mind. "Give me the flashgun."

"Are you..." she shoots into the pile of dead things. "...fucking crazy? Do you even know how to shoot one?"

"No. But it might be our only chan—"

A loud, reverberating shriek cuts through everything. Even the beasts fall silent. Gerty half turns, rifle barrel smoldering.

The shrieking noise grows louder as the gate shakes, then shudders upward. It's about thirty inches from the floor, then shivers to a stop.

Gerty faces the dead pile and shoots anything that moves. Over the gunfire she shouts, "Your call, Alyx!"

But she's already calculating. Thirty is more than enough for either of them to fit under without their packs and gear.

This next part is the trickiest. They need enough time to scoot their packs under and shimmy under the gate before the beasts can catch them. But there's also another hitch. Once they make it out, how are they going to keep the creatures from following?

As Alyx shrugs off her pack, she hopes there's another keyhole on the other side. If not, well...

"Toss me your packs," she tells Gerty.

"What?"

"Just toss them to me."

Gerty manages the task, and sets the packs aside, not really able to toss them and keep her focus on the dead pile of creatures as the living ones try eating their way through like rats. Alyx retrieves the packs, one of them containing the ashes of the fallen soldiers, including Row and Rip. She runs to the partially open gate and shoves all the packs through.

She shouts, "*Now*. Run as fast as you can!"

Gerty fires off the riffle in crisscrossing pattern, then bolts toward the gate.

"Run," Alyx shouts.

Gerty slides under the opening of the gate to the other side and Alyx yanks the artifact out of the keyhole. The floor once more begins to quake. The grinding sounds within the wall erupt. The gate quivers and begins to lower.

"*Alyx*," Gerty nearly screams from the other side.

Enough is enough. Alyx sprints to the gate just as the remaining creatures break through their dead brethren and scramble after her.

She slides under the gate, losing her John Deere cap in the process.

She pats her head, eyes wide. "Shit."

Inches before the gate slams home, she reaches under, snatches her cap and yanks it to the other side with her. Dust plumes as the gate settles back into the floor.

Alyx snugs the cap on her head and rolls away from the metal bars.

The creatures slam into the gate, growling and snapping their toothed maws. Long claws curl around the bars. But they can't get through.

Gerty helps Alyx to her feet. "You really risked an arm for that hat?" Gerty chuckles.

"It's good luck."

They blink at each other for a moment, then both burst into laughter. On the other side of the gate, the beasts bellow and whine...and eventually begin to howl.

TWENTY-ONE

"Holy shit," Connors manages through breaths as they round the corner. "Thought I'd never see you guys again. I..." He frowns. "Where's everybody else?"

Gerty sighs. "Dead. C'mon, man. Let's get topside."

Hustling to keep up, Connors says, "What happened in there?"

Alyx grunts. "Bad things."

"Like what?"

"Let's just put it this way, kid." Alyx manages a ghost of a smile. "You were the smart one to stay outside."

Connors's freckled face wrinkles in a deep frown. "When that door closed, I...I tried opening it again but couldn't find a way."

Alyx nods. "It's okay." She makes sure the artifact is secure in the pack and sets her attention to the tunnels above. "We have bigger fish to fry anyway."

"Bigger fish to...*what*?"

Alyx, still staring at the tunnels, shakes her head. "Never mind."

And, just as she assumed, there's a way to bring the step back and reenter the tunnels. Much to Gerty's dismay.

The venture back, however isn't as treacherous as the first time through.

At least until the end.

TWENTY-TWO

The man standing in front of the steps leading topside isn't one of the men Vilas sent with the rest of the team. No, this guy is much larger...and he's holding a grenade launcher.

"Halt," this behemoth bellows.

Alyx stops the other two and says, "We're what's left of the exploration."

"Dr. Wick? Is there a Dr. Sullivan with you?"

"He is."

The man cocks his head to the right, as if listening to something only he can hear. "Dr. Sullivan is older. From what I see there are two women and a scrawny boy."

"Well, I didn't say he was with us in the flesh, asshole, now did I?"

He points the grenade launcher at Alyx. "Sweet dreams, bitch."

"What if I said I have the artifact?"

The large man cocks his head to the right again.

"Is that like a nervous tick or something?" Gerty whispers and Alyx restrains a giggle.

"Let me see it," the man says.

"Then put that damn gun down and let me show you," Alyx says.

The man lowers the gun, though not entirely.

Still, Alyx brings it out of the pack and holds it up. "Let us pass."

Once more, the man cocks his head.

Then Alyx gets it. She turns to Gerty. "He's an android. Every time he cocks his head like that, he's receiving new information."

"How do you even know that?"

Alyx shrugs. "I don't. But it makes sense."

"Or he's just got a nervous tick like you said, Gerty," Connor says.

Both women give him an exasperated glance. Gerty says to Alyx, "So what's your plan?"

"Shoot him. Because next he'll probably ask for me to hand it over. And if I do, he'll shoot me and both of you."

"And what if he's human?"

"I really don't care at this point," Alyx says. "He'll shoot us no matter if he's human or not. Vilas is footing the bill and—"

"Give me the artifact and I'll take you to see Vilas," the large man says.

Alyx tips Gerty a wink and the girl rolls her eyes.

Holding the artifact up with her left hand, she starts forward. "Okay. We just want to get off this planet now. Vilas can have the damn artifact."

The man cocks his head. When he straightens he says, "Very well. You will be transported back home by the rescue squad."

"Sounds good." She's about fifteen feet away from him now.

"That's far enough," the man says. "Place the artifact on the ground and return to your friends."

Alyx stops, still holding the artifact up. "I thought we were going to be transported?"

The huge man nods. "And you will. But first I need to authenticate the artifact."

She stoops to place the artifact on the tunnel's floor, and in one fluid motion draws her revolver and shoots out his left knee. The man drops, making an audible grunt. He lifts the grenade launcher.

"Shit," Gerty shouts. "Run!"

Alyx points her gun at the man, pulls the trigger. *Click.*

She stares at the gun stupidly for a split-second, realizing it's empty. Because of course it is. Any time she truly needs the damn thing it's always out of bullets. Along her belt are the remaining six. Her backup when time is critical.

Alyx manages to load a single bullet when the man says, "Last chance. Place the artifact on the ground and step back, or you're dead."

"Alyx," Gerty says.

But she ignores the girl, slams the cylinder home, aims the revolver and squeezes the trigger a moment before the man fully lifts the grenade launcher. In less than a blink a large portion of his face disappears, splattering the air with a strange, greenish liquid. The man's head cocks to the right, jitters there, then slams to the left. The launcher rises and falls, rises and falls.

She hears the gun blast a second before the man's head explodes in a glut of goo. His body jerks, lurches, falls flat as the pale green liquid spurts from the stump of its neck. The launcher, still in his hand, clacks against the stone floor as his body stills.

Gerty pats Alyx's shoulder as she brushes by, gun barrel smoking. "Got your back, babe."

Alyx stares after her, swallows. "Thanks." The word comes out in a breathless tone. The man would've killed them all if Gerty hadn't acted. There was no way Alyx could load another bullet before he fired.

They stand around the headless thing. Connors picks up the grenade launcher and slings it over his shoulder, almost as an afterthought Alyx notes.

"Android," Gerty says and kicks the AI's side. It doesn't move.

"Didn't I say—"

Gerty waves a dismissive hand. "Yeah, yeah. I know. How about we go kick some ass now, okay?"

Alyx smirks. "Damn right."

They hurry up the steps leading topside and all Alyx can think about is punching Valis's wrinkly, smug face in.

But the moment they emerge from the tunnels, the land is utterly deserted. All gray rock and nothing else. A complete wasteland as it had been before.

Gerty sucks in deep breaths of relatively fresh air and blows them out. She smiles. "Finally." She glances around. "Where is he?"

Alyx stares off toward the woods. "We need to move. Now. I think Hannah is in danger."

"Hannah? But why would he...?"

"Because he wants a way off this rock," Alyx says. "The rescue team is either dead or sent away. He wants to look like the hero in all this."

A shrill squealing noise startles them all and it doesn't take long for Alyx to realize it's coming from her pack. Within the squealing, she thinks she hears a voice.

Pulling out the voice recorder, the transmit symbol blinks sporadically. On the screen, it reads, VILAS.

Alyx steels herself, and touches the answer icon on the screen.

"—Sullivan! Come in Dr. White!"

"This is Alyx, dickhead. Sully is dead."

There's a moment of silence, then Vilas says, "Dead? How? What the *hell* is going on?"

"Oh don't play dumb. I know you had him swindled."

"Our deal was solid, I assure you. Especially regarding his daughter. I was doing the right thing Alyx."

"Right. You were playing him. As soon as you got the artifact in your hands you would have killed him. I know you, Vilas." There's so much rage now, she just wants to smash the voice recorder on the ground. Instead, her grip tightens around it. "How are Lance and Hannah doing?"

"You think you know me, but in reality, you've fabricated some twisted fantasy. I am not a bad guy, Alyx, just did some bad things, like you have. I have morals. I have respect for those I choose to help. Lance and Hannah are well. The cruiser is just about tip-top shape."

Alyx chuckles humorlessly. "You've never helped anybody but yourself."

"And how do you know this for sure? I keep my private deals private. Dr. Sullivan and I had a private deal. He brings me the artifact, I pay for his daughter's treatments until she is cured." He pauses. "Did you recover the artifact?"

Alyx grins. "You'll have to see to find out."

Once more, he pauses. After a moment, he says, "There are three gliders resting at the edge of the woods. Each one is set for my location. Bring me the artifact and I'll make a new deal with you."

"Out," Alyx says and turns the voice recorder off. She stuffs it in the pack and looks at Gerty and Connors. "It's going to be a free for all once we reach Vilas. He wants the artifact and will do everything he can to get it. He'll be ready for us and it's more than likely he'll shoot us off our gliders and collect the artifact than actually try to talk me out of it."

"So, what should we do?" Gerty asks. "I mean, we can't just charge in, guns blazing. He has men, or androids, or whatever the hell they are."

"We park the gliders away from the cruiser where he's waiting. I'm sure he has tracking on them. Then we each take a point around them. Connors, you use that grenade launcher to blow up his tracker."

"His what?"

"Tracker. A big silver thing on wheels. Just don't shoot the cruiser."

Connors nods.

"Gerty, I want you to pick off all the men standing guard while I go in to take out Vilas."

"You're like the most badass teacher ever."

Alyx shakes her head, laughing. "Let's do this. And if things go wrong, seize the cruiser and get the hell out of here. With or without me."

Neither Gerty or Connors says anything to this and they all hurry to find the gliders.

TWENTY-THREE

They're on the gliders, slipping through the wood on a course set by Vilas and Alyx turns the situation over in her mind while keeping a close eye out for any creatures lurking about.

A wide strip has been cut out of the forest making it easier on the gliders, but...

Vilas just has to destroy things. Doesn't matter what it is, he must destroy it in some way.

There isn't a map or anything on the gliders so she eventually needs to pay attention to her surroundings and remember what the woods looked like when they first entered it. All she really remembers is how dense it was. How thick the foliage was.

The one thing she does remember is how long it took to get from point A to point B.

About two hours or so. Give or take.

And they've been on the gliders for a little over an hour, she figures.

Alyx glares ahead as Gerty and Connors flank her on either side. She's so focused, she doesn't see the creatures hanging from the trees. Doesn't even realize what's going on until it's too late.

An ambush.

The ape-like creatures drop onto them with so much force they slam Alyx, Gerty and Connors off the gliders. Alyx lands hard, skidding into a tree and taking the brunt of the force with her left shoulder. A muffled pop and agony spreads through her. She rolls onto her right side, teeth gritting against the pain.

Shrill gibbering noises fill her ears.

"Alyx," Gerty shouts. "Where are you?"

Alyx manages to sit and yells, "Over here."

A long burst of chattering gunfire ignites the woods, then Gerty crashes through a set of thick bushes, Connors in tow. They help her to her feet and she bites back a cry as pain lashes through her shoulder. Her left arm dangles at her side like a dead snake.

"You're hurt," Gerty says, frowning.

"Yeah. Shoulder is dislocated I think."

Connors steps forward. "Mine dislocates all the time. I can help."

All around them, shrill gibbering. Bluish leaves see-saw down from the trees above. A shiver scuttles under Alyx's skin.

"I only have one magazine left," Gerty says. "The flashgun is too slow for an ambush like this."

As Connors inspects Alyx's shoulder, she says, "Start a fire."

"A...fire?"

With Connors rubbing around her shoulder, as pain ladders down her back, Alyx nods. "In the trees. Maybe it'll scare them off."

"But won't we be in danger? I mean...a forest fire is kind of extreme."

Connors yanks sharply downward on Alyx's arm. Another muffled pop as her shoulder slips back into its socket, then all she knows is white, hot agony for a few seconds. Once this subsides, a dull ache radiates throughout her shoulder, back and left arm. But, at least she can move her arm now. Kind of. Feels too weak. Too slow.

When she regains her composure, she points at the grenades clipped to Connors's belt. "Two of those are flash grenades. We run and light up the forest behind us. We need all the ammo we can save for Vilas."

Gerty shakes her head. "I forget how crazy you are sometimes." She sighs. "But okay. Let's do this."

Above, Alyx catches a glimpse of a wiry, hairless, dark shape move through the branches. Blue leaves sift to the ground.

"Connors," she says. "As soon as Gerty and I take off, throw a flash grenade as high as you can into the tree. The initial flash might scare them off too. But as soon as you throw it, follow us. If you notice the things not reacting, throw another grenade at a tree."

Connors, face dripping with sweat and blood from a small gash in his forehead, nods without argument.

Alyx turns to Gerty, "Only shoot if you have to."

"Ya know," Gerty says. "I *am* the next in command, right?"

Alyx smiles. "Right."

Gerty shakes her head. "Okay, let's do this already."

"Run," Alyx says.

Gerty and Alyx sprint away from Connors and instantly the shrill gibbering noises turn to raspy hoots. The creatures are warning each other about the escape attempt. And they're pissed off about it, apparently.

A moment after the women are running, a loud crack echoes through the woods. The hoots change to screams.

Alyx glances over her shoulder. Connors isn't far behind.

She just hopes she's right and the fire scares the things away.

She hopes.

TWENTY-FOUR

She catches a whiff of smoke, but it's minor. Nothing strong enough to worry her too much. The entire forest will probably catch, but by that time Vilas will be neutralized and they'll be on their way home.

At least that's the plan.

Connors, huffing and puffing from all the running, manages, "They retreated."

Alyx, also trying to breathe, manages a nod.

Gerty, she runs headstrong through the cleared path Vilas created. There are no signs of the gliders and Alyx assumes they continued on to their programmed destination.

Nothing appears the same as it had when they first entered the woods, so Alyx has no way of fully knowing how close they are.

Finally, she slows her pace and says, "Save…your energy."

The two Marines don't argue and slow to a walk. Neither of them are breathing as heavily as Alyx and she hates herself for not keeping in shape over the years.

Once all their breathing eases, Gerty says, "So we lost our gliders and just started a forest fire." She snorts. "Well, at least we're not trapped in a sacrificial temple or something."

Alyx chuckles. "There's that. I think we're getting close now."

"Yeah." Gerty points at a large tree with black vines choking its thick trunk. "I remember that and I don't think we were too far in when I spotted it. Thought the tree looked like it was in pain."

"It does," Alyx says. "Okay, so let's be ready. But I'm banking on the gliders showing up to Vilas empty and him thinking we all died back there. He'll send men out to retrieve the artifact."

"I smell ambush," Gerty sings and cackles all witch-like.

"Exactly," Alyx says and cocks a thumb at Connors. "But he'll be doing most of the shooting."

Connors blinks. "Huh?"

"The grenade launcher. It'll save ammo if they're in a group and blow them to bits."

"That's dark, dude," Gerty says, though she's grinning.

Ahead, there's a small clearing where the trees and foliage open nice and wide. Wide enough, anyway. To the right of this clearing, the land slopes upward into a gradual hill.

"Connors, I think if you stand on the hill there you'll get the best vantage point to pick the perfect shot."

"You sure you were never in the military, Professor?" Gerty winks.

"I wouldn't last two hours as a soldier," Alyx says, not feeding into Gerty's playful nature. She's getting too focused now. "But a hill is the highest point. And according to history, hills gain the upper hand in any ambush." She grunts. "Or trees…"

"So serious," Gerty spouts, and falls silent as Connors hustles toward the hill with his grenade launcher.

Gerty and Alyx crouch in the thick brush near the foot of the small hill.

The wait isn't long. About ten minutes or so, telling Alyx all she needs to know about how far away Vilas is.

The men enter the clearing in a group, just as she hoped. No stragglers as far as she can tell.

Boom.

One moment they're there, the next…a splatterfest. Also…

"They're all droids," Gerty says as she steps into the clearing.

Connors makes his way down the hill, all wide-eyed, but smiling. He did good, and he knows it.

"Because actual humans would probably turn on Vilas," Alyx says. An assumption, but probably a good one.

There's barely anything left of the droids, and what does remain are bits and pieces. Arms. Legs. A charred head opens and closes its mouth, eyes darting back and forth. Alyx puts a bullet in it.

"Let's go." She walks out of the clearing, setting her sights ahead.

It's time to end this.

TWNETY-FIVE

The problem is, Vilas's tracker is parked in front of the cruiser. So, no matter how much Alyx wants to blow the damn thing up, she can't risk damaging the cruiser.

Three man-droids stand near it, each one slowly scanning the perimeter.

There's no sign of Vilas, Lance, or Hannah. Besides the man-droids, the large clearing is still and silent.

Gerty and Alyx back away from the nearest bushes.

"If that's all that's left of his little army," Gerty says, "I can take them out no problem."

Alyx nods. "Yeah, but it could also be a trap. Vilas is an asshole like that."

"He'd still be on edge after thinking we're dead?"

"Maybe. But I wouldn't put it past him."

Gerty shrugs, lifts Rip's rifle. "I say fuck it. Let's see what happens."

Smiling, Alyx says, "If things turn to shit out there, I want to thank you. You did more than you needed to for everyone, including me."

"Pshhh, I just didn't want to be stuck in those tunnels alone." But Gerty smiles back and pats Alyx's arm. "You're good people, Dr. Wick."

Alyx turns to Connors. "If you don't get promoted after this, I'll personally kick General Hunt in the fluff."

Connor snorts, shakes his head. "It's an honor just being here. But thanks, Dr. Wick." His face goes a little dim. "Just wish my platoon was still here with us."

"Same," Gerty says, then sighs. "But they're not, so let's honor our fallen by kicking some major ass. What do ya say, bro?"

Connors grins, lifts his sidearm. "Oorah."

Gerty claps the kid on the back and all three burst out of the brush, guns blazing.

In no time, the three man-droids are reduced to jittering, oozing things in the dirt. Alyx and Gerty open the back of the tracker while Connors keeps watch.

Both women stumble back, faces pinched to the godawful reek washing out of the bus-like vehicle.

"Jesus," Gerty says, touching the collar of her vest. The mask shoots up and melds to her mouth and nose.

Alyx follows suit. Instantly, the stench is gone.

They creep into the vehicle, shoulder lights illuminating the darkness. A gurgling groan drifts to Alyx's ears and...

"Oh my god," Alyx says, barely able to breathe.

On a large, steel table, Lance turns his head and spurts vomit onto the floor where it splatters in a rancid pool of the same.

"L-Lance?" Gerty starts forward, stops.

He doesn't seem to notice, coughs and his head lolls back and forth. But it's not the pool of vomit on the floor, or him being naked, nor the stench that sends slivers of ice into Alyx's chest.

No. It's how his stomach bulges outward, as if he's nine months pregnant. It's the black veins snaking just under the stretched skin. It's how that considerable belly shifts and makes low groaning sounds. It's the wires and tubes running in and out of both of his arms to monitors and machines she's never seen before. All of them are dark. All of them shutdown.

What the hell was Vilas up to in here?

"I'd advise you two to step out of the tracker and shut the door," Vilas's soothing voice says. "He's critical."

Alyx spins, all her hate pushing to the surface. "What the *fuck* did you do, Vilas? What the hell is going on here?"

The older man frowns. "What did I—my dear, I have done nothing to this poor boy. He was infected by that thing in the tunnel. I tried everything I could to reverse his condition. But, as you can see, my efforts were in vain."

"You can drop the act now," Alyx says, hand falling to the butt of her revolver. With only four bullets left, she hopes Vilas is alone.

Vilas looks genuinely hurt by the comment. His face slackens, gaze lowers a bit. "I suppose I deserve that for what I've done to you over the years."

"Damn right you do. You stole some of my most priceless finds."

"And tell me," his gaze returns to her, "what were your plans for those priceless finds? Those artifacts and crystals, and rare metals. Hmm?" And when Alyx can't think of anything to say, he nods. "You and I are not so much different from each other, Alyx. You robbed from the dead to sell to the highest bidder. And I robbed you to do the same."

"Whoa," Gerty says. "You're more messed up than I thought."

Alyx sighs. "I was trying to retire."

"Retire? Aren't you like thirty-five?"

"Thirty-three, but that's beside the point."

"Not really, but whatever. He's right." Gerty steps away from Alyx. "You're just as bad as he is. You're both thieves."

"You see," Vilas says, that smug smile finally surfacing. "Sooner or later, all our demons come out to play."

"He's trying to turn you against me," Alyx says to Gerty. "I sold to *museums* mostly. Not black-market buyers like he does."

Gerty glances from Alyx to Vilas and back again. "And that makes you better than him?"

"No, but at least the things I have found can be enjoyed by others and not hoarded in a room by some rich collector."

Before she speaks again, Gerty dips her a wink. "Wrong. It makes you the same, and I want you to stay right where you are. I'm going to find Hannah and we're getting off this fucking rock." She points her rifle at Vilas. "And you, get the hell out of my way."

Vilas puts his hands up, smiling. "Of course, young lady. Hannah is in the cruiser if you wish to speak with her."

Gerty shoots Alyx a firm expression Alyx interprets as, "Get ready", and storms out of the tracker. Vilas lets her pass without a word. Then the woman Marine disappears around the side of the tracker. Where Connors is at, she doesn't know.

Behind her, Lance's extended stomach gurgles and groans.

Her focus fixes on Vilas. He's smiling, though there seems something a bit different. The smugness isn't as prominent. And after a few seconds, he sighs.

"I am truly sorry for your loss, Alyx. Dr. White was a great man. He said he was ill, but I didn't know how ill. And you must believe me that my involvement here is strictly to help his daughter."

And...she kind of does believe him. She doesn't want to. She wants to shoot him. But then again, what if she's been misjudging him this entire time on the planet? What if he's really here to help and not take for himself?

"So, what now?" she asks, probing a bit. "Now that Sully is dead, I suppose you're going to take the artifact and sell it to the highest bidder?"

Vilas shakes his head. "The deal is broken, I don't even want the artifact now. I mean, look at me, Alyx. Take a serious look. I have no real friends. I am an old man obsessed with wealth. I have it all, yet nothing."

"That was your choice. All those times you stole from me..."

"Yes," Vilas says. "And I hope you can forgive me for that. Though would you believe my life had grown so dull that I actually looked forward to our little encounters? You, Alyx, gave an old, tired man purpose again."

Alyx lifts an eyebrow. "You drunk?"

Vilas chuckles. "Not at all. And see! This is exactly the sort of excitement I need. This fire in you burns me and I absolutely can't get enough."

"That's pretty creepy, even for you."

He waves a hand. "Not anything sexual. You've just brought meaning to my life."

"Great. Fantastic. Can I have all the money you sold my finds for now?"

But his gaze shifts away. "I had a wife once. Long time ago. I have a son too. Rory, his name is. Haven't seen him in twenty-five years. Such a long time. She remarried, of course. And I'm sure she never told him who his father really is. But, you know, I've observed them. They are a happy family. Rory is well and has a wife of his own now. He is happy. And that's all a father really wants for his children, isn't it? Happiness."

Behind her, an oddly wet ripping sound steals Alyx's hearing.

And, for just a split-second, that smug smile surfaces on Vilas's face. There and gone, but she catches it a moment before she turns around.

Lance's stomach splits open, spewing hundreds of small worm-like creatures. Stark white, about five inches long, they spill out of Lance onto the floor and wriggle toward her in vigorous slithers.

Alyx stumbles backward, trips over her own feet and lands hard on the ground outside the tracker. All the wind whooshes out of her lungs.

Vilas grins down at her. "Although all I have told is very true, there is one thing I forgot to mention, Alyx. I'm not here for the artifact or Dr. White's daughter. I'm here for these lovely beings."

Tiny chittering noise grows closer and closer.

"You see, artifacts, metal and gems, all of that, it's all nothing compared to life, Alyx. *Life*. These creatures will sell for millions each to scientists, alien enthusiasts and collectors. Top buyers all over the galaxy." His smile loses the smugness. "I really am not a bad guy, and I truly did plan on paying Dr. White for the artifact. I am not heartless, after all. But you see...I can't leave this planet without those creatures. And once they burrow into you, they'll feed off your insides until we are home. You'll need to be transported in a secure pod, of course."

"You're insane," Alyx says once she catches her breath.

"Insane?" Vilas laughs a bit. "No. This is smart business, Alyx. Something you should learn if you ever want that early retirement you so long for. Not that you have to worry about any of that now because—"

Thunk. Vilas's eyes pop open wide, then his eyelids flutter. He sways then a hand shoves him out of the way.

Connors helps her to her feet. "Thought he was a good guy at first. Sorry I took so long."

"Better late than never. Thanks." She turns, watches the worm things plop onto the ground and quickly steps away. "Where's Gerty?"

"She's been in the cruiser most of the time."

On the ground, Vilas moans, rolls onto his back, blinking. He touches the bloody spot on the side of his head and sucks in a sharp breath. The worm things slither toward him. Their chittering fills the silent void.

"Hey, Vilas," Alyx says.

He blinks, squints at her.

"Not that you have to worry about it, but…" she points at the worm-like creatures.

Vilas's eyes widen, he jerks his head to the right just as a swarm of the worms slither like snakes onto him. He screams as they burrow their way into his body.

Alyx grimaces watching the worms eat their way into the old man, and turns away.

"Let's get the hell out of here," she says.

Alyx leads the way to the cruiser's open back hatch. "Gerty?"

The hyper sleep area is deserted. Likewise, the small kitchen.

She's at the bridge's door when Connors says, "Before you open the door, there's something you should know."

Alyx, pulling the latch, sighs. "What is it?"

There's a faint click behind her. "Vilas was my father."

Her heart stutters. "*Rory?*"

"Connors is my step-dad's name."

Her hand falls to the butt of the revolver.

"Ah-ah," Rory says. "Hands up, Dr. Wick."

She slowly lifts her hands up.

"Now turn around. I need your help."

Alyx faces him. "My help for what?"

He smiles, and it's so close to Vilas's smug grin her stomach churns seeing it. "We need to load my father in a secure pod for our way back home."

"You can't—are you *serious*?"

"Very serious. My father was an asshole. You're right about that. But, he was a smart asshole. And I was banking on him arriving here eventually."

"Rory, look," Alyx says. "His plan will probably make you very rich, but at what cost? If those things spread…"

"Oh, they won't. They're all going to one buyer for the highest dollar. You've been a good person, Dr. Wick. You saved the day. But, my mother and I need this payday for what he did to us."

Alyx frowns. "Did to you?"

"Oh come on, you really believed all of that about my mother and I? Mom didn't leave him, he was *cheating* on her. He kicked us out. Only later did he try to reconnect and by then I hated him. So, in a way, stealing the business from him is like the ultimate payback."

"How will you keep them contained? If the buyer doesn't—"

"Enough, Dr. Wick. You will help me load him up and when we return home, you'll promise to make sure of his safe arrival to my buyer. There's no way around this. I'm sorry, but I've been planning this for a long time and I won't be—"

Behind Alyx, the door clicks.

Rory's gaze shifts over Alyx's shoulder.

It's all she needs.

Alyx lunges, grabs the sidearm, twisting it out of his hand. She has a second or two of triumph before he slaps the gun out of her hand and sucker punches her in the stomach, driving all the wind out of her. She crumples to her knees, trying to breathe. She manages a sip of air, a gulp, then she straightens with an uppercut to the young man's chin. He stumbles back, eyes rolling back in their sockets. Blood trickles from the corner of his mouth. He catches his balance, shakes his head and glares at Alyx.

Then he roars, leaping at her, fists flying. One of these fists clips her left ear sending a flare of pain. She shoves him away, slams her boot into a knee as hard as she can. There's a meaty snap and Rory's leg folds in the wrong direction. He screams, drops to the floor of the cruiser. Alyx kicks the sidearm away and presses the muzzle of her revolver to Rory's forehead. He wails, holding his damaged leg.

"Holy shit, what the hell is going on here?"

Alyx says, "Gerty, meet Vilas's son, Rory."

The young man rolls on the floor, wailing and sobbing from all the pain.

"Jesus," Gerty says. "I leave you alone for five minutes and all hell breaks loose."

"It's been fun," Alyx says. "But I think it's time we get off this dead world."

"Well, technically it's not dead, Alyx. I mean—ohhh, you mean because everyone keeps dying here."

Alyx sighs. "Yeah. Something like that."

Another woman says, "We'll be taking off in about five minutes. Everyone get strapped in. Once we get out of orbit, I'll set the course."

"Hi, Hannah," Alyx says without taking her sight off Rory.

He's crying now, but at least the wailing has subsided.

"Hi, Dr. Wick," Hannah says. "Five minutes, guys. If you're not strapped in, you'll be tossed everywhere."

"Okay," Gerty says. Then to Alyx. "So, what are we gonna do with this dude?"

Alyx smiles.

TWENTY-SIX

With Rory fast asleep in a secure pod, Alyx and Gerty buckle into seats as the cruiser rises off the planet and into orbit.

Once everything stabilizes, Hannah emerges from the bridge and says, "Okay. Course is set. We better get to hyper sleep."

"Thanks, Hannah," Alyx says.

"Yeah, I just wish everyone was coming back with us."

Alyx pats her pack. "In a way, they are." She kicks herself for not gathering Lance's ashes, but things got too crazy too fast.

Hannah nods, on the verge of tears. Gerty gives her a hug. Once Hannah is done crying, she gently pushes Gerty away and says, "Let's get to hyper sleep."

"Whatever happened to the rescue team, by the way?" Alyx asks, unbuckling her seatbelt.

Hannah lowers her head. "Vilas incinerated them."

"Damn."

There's a long moment of silence for all the fallen, then Gerty straightens. "They'll all be honored at Base."

Hannah and Gerty wander off toward the hyper sleep chambers and Alyx watches them go.

She sits for a while, staring at nothing and thinking about Sully.

She brings the artifact out of her pack and holds it up, gaze slipping over all the pits in the stone and intricate carvings covering it.

A smile slowly spreads along her face.

TWENTY-SEVEN

The young woman, somewhere in her middle twenties, drops the note onto her lap and sobs into her withered hands. On the table beside her bed is a silver suitcase sitting open and filled with stacks of money.

Alyx Wick detaches herself from the doorway, turns and walks out of the hospital.

The sun is bright and warm this day and she stops on the sidewalk, turning her face toward it. She lets the warmth soak into her bruised skin and after a moment, she continues on her way.

Memories of Sully flicker through her mind and she can't help but smile.

And she thinks, as she works her way toward her apartment across town, *For you, Sully. For you. She's going to be okay now, my dear friend.*

A dull rumble sounds in the distance and her gaze lifts to the horizon where dark clouds billow and churn.

The smile on her face fades a little.

There's a storm coming.

Because, sometimes, there is no happiness without darkness.

And, sometimes, even if there is life, worlds die.

THE END

CHECK OUT OTHER GREAT SCIENCE FICTION BOOKS

ROAK
by Jake Bible

There are thousands of bounty hunters across the galaxy. Solid professionals that take jobs based on the credits the bounties afford. They follow the letter of the law so they can maximize those credits.

Licensed, bonded, legal.

Then there's Roak.

Deadly, unstoppable, invisible.

SIEGE
by Gustavo Bondoni

This is humanity's last stand. Threatened on all sides by enemies they can't fight and often can't even comprehend, the human race has taken refuge in an inhospitable corner of the galaxy. A tiny pocket of habitable space concealed by black holes and dust clouds, hiding a cluster of colonies where the last humans in the galaxy reside, preparing themselves for a war of annihilation against all comers. Crystallia is a hidden military base that guards the access route to the colonies. The main mission of the soldiers there is to remain undetected for as long as possible, to spot any incursions from the outside and to hit them with everything in humanity's arsenal. No one is quite convinced that this strategy will be enough to save the colonies or even to create enough of a delay for some of the colonists to escape. The best bet for the human race is to remain concealed. Unfortunately, something has found them.

CHECK OUT OTHER GREAT SCIENCE FICTION BOOKS

MAUSOLEUM 2069
by **Rick Jones**

Political dignitaries including the President of the Federation gather for a ceremony onboard Mausoleum 2069. But when a cloud of interstellar dust passes through the galaxy and eclipses Earth, the tenants within the walls of Mausoleum 2069 are reborn and the undead begin to rise. As the struggle between life and death onboard the mausoleum develops, Eriq Wyman, a one-time member of a Special ops team called the Force Elite, is given the task to lead the President to the safety of Earth. But is Earth like Mausoleum 2069? A landscape of the living dead? Has the war of the Apocalypse finally begun? With so many questions there is only one certainty: in space there is nowhere to run and nowhere to hide.

RED CARBON
by **D.J. Goodman**

Diamonds have been discovered on Mars.

After years of neglect to space programs around the world, a ruthless corporation has made it to the Red Planet first, establishing their own mining operation with its own rules and laws, its own class system, and little oversight from Earth. Conditions are harsh, but its people have learned how to make the Martian colony home.

But something has gone catastrophically wrong on Earth. As the colony leaders try to cover it up, hacker Leah Hartnup is getting suspicious. Her boundless curiosity will lead her to a horrifying truth: they are cut off, possibly forever. There are no more supplies coming. There will be no more support. There is no more mission to accomplish. All that's left is one goal: survival.

CHECK OUT OTHER GREAT SCIENCE FICTION BOOKS

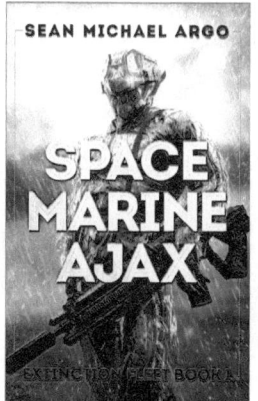

SPACE MARINE AJAX
by Sean-Michael Argo

Ajax answers the call of duty and becomes an Einherjar space marine, charged with defending humanity against hideous alien monsters in furious combat across the galaxy.

The Garm, as they came to be called, emerged from the deepest parts of uncharted space, devouring all that lay before them, a great swarm that scoured entire star systems of all organic life. This space borne hive, this extinction fleet, made no attempts to communicate and offered no mercy.

Humanity has always been a deadly organism, and we would not so easily be made the prey. Unified against a common enemy, we fought back, meeting the swarm with soldiers upon every front.

PLANET LEVIATHAN
by D.J. Goodman

The cyborg commandos of the Galactic Marines are the greatest warriors in the galaxy, but sometimes one will go bad. Too unstable to be let back into the general population and too powerful for a normal prison to hold them, there is only one place they can be sent: Planet Leviathan.

www.ingramcontent.com/pod-product-compliance
Lightning Source LLC
Chambersburg PA
CBHW021959190626
46808CB00017B/2569